To Amy, whose love and strength powered this ship.

SPACE RIOT

PAT SHAND

JOE BOOKS LTD

Published simultaneously in the United States and Canada
by Joe Books Ltd, 489 College Street, Toronto, ON M6G 1A5

www.joebooks.com

Library and Archives Canada Cataloguing in Publication
information is available upon request

ISBN 978-1-77275-334-9 (print)
ISBN 978-1-77275-537-4 (ebook)

First Joe Books edition: May 2017

MARVEL

Printed and bound in Canada
1 3 5 7 9 10 8 6 4 2

CHAPTER ONE

A Pit Stop on Putriline

Star-Lord

"Okay, so here are the options," said Peter Quill, known across the universe as Star-Lord by friends and enemies alike (but mostly by enemies), as he stood before the battalion of quivering, green-grey masses. The creatures were holding on to a trio of crates worth more than the collective goods the planet he was currently docked upon had to offer. Granted, said planet—which appeared on Star-Lord's map as "Putriline" but was pronounced by its natives as a sort of sloshing noise that sounded to Star-Lord like someone without teeth chewing loudly on mashed potatoes—was not known for its abundance of wealth. As far as the spacefaring renegade—an epithet that Star-Lord had to admit no one had ever used to describe him—could tell, Putriline was little more than a ball of moss suspended near the edge of charted space. Its sole impressive feature: it was spotted with a great number of deep craters, which made the planet look to Star-Lord like a loofah.

Be that as it may, those quivering, green-grey masses had

managed to get the jump on Star-Lord and his crew, the Guardians of the Galaxy. The aliens had lulled the team into a false sense of security, separated them, and stolen the packages they were en route to deliver, which Quill had to admit was a little funny, given the team's name. The galaxy? Yeah, they'd guard the crap out of that. A bunch of crates, though, *that* was a tall order.

They hadn't expected trouble like this when they first landed, though. Putriline was the final planet before the last leg of their trip, so the team had stopped to fill up for the final run. The gelatinous aliens had initially seemed rather pleasant, despite how little of their sloshy language the Guardians understood—but that wasn't generally a problem for a team that included a walking tree named Groot who had never really gotten the whole talking thing down, and Rocket, an anthropomorphic raccoon that spoke mostly in a string of profanity. After the crew was done refueling, they kicked back in a tavern that, while it *did* smell like Rocket's dirty laundry, offered perhaps the most potent ale any of them had ever tasted.

Turns out, there was a reason the Putrilines hadn't been drinking with them.

When Star-Lord awoke in the tavern basement, his hands were bound by a glob of slime, his friends were nowhere to be found, and what felt like tiny hammers were having an all-night dance party in his skull. He managed to break free of the goo, which even now left a layer of stickiness on his hands, and ran outside and across a stretch of moss just in time to see the Putrilines unloading the cargo from the *Milano*, Star-Lord's beautiful spaceship named for an equally beautiful television actress he had been fond of during his days on Earth.

Star-Lord's life was awesome, but he couldn't deny it—he missed the hell out of TV.

Now, as he put on his most menacing strut-and-glare—a patented move—Star-Lord noted that all of his weapons had been taken except for his battle helmet, which was a blessing, as the planet's atmosphere would have set his lungs on fire the moment it was removed. The helmet was currently closed, masking the whole of Star-Lord's face and hiding his glare behind two burning, red circles, which he hoped looked menacing to the Putrilines on this dark, hazy night.

"Option one," Star-Lord said, his worn, crimson cloak billowing behind him as the wind caught it. Behind the mask, he allowed himself a brief smile—the cloak billow was a good touch, nice and dramatic. "You piles of snot drop the crates, super careful-like, and back up. Way, way up. If you think you've backed up far enough? Nope. Keep backing."

The Putrilines looked at him, some of them cocking their quivering heads, gripping the crates.

"Right, I guess you want to hear the other options," Star-Lord said, taking a step toward the creatures. "Totally get it. Option two! Say you *don't* give up the boxes. You, for whatever reason, figure you can use what we've got in there. Ransack the ship, take what we got, maybe sell it on the black market to anyone who can understand what you're saying—which, good luck, dudes—but let's tackle one problem at a time. If you do that, I'm going to have an issue. And when I have an issue, I get anxious. And when I get anxious, I start shooting things. Especially things that look like a bowl of Jell-O got up and started walking around."

The Putrilines inclined their heads at each other, doing whatever was the slime-puddle equivalent of a glance. After deliberating between themselves with a few mushy sounds, they turned back to Star-Lord, their hold on the boxes tight as ever.

"All right," Star-Lord said, advancing once again. They didn't back up. "Third option. You might notice the trend here, which is that we started in a good place with our options, went to a not-so-good place, and now . . . can anyone guess where we're going? Good place again? Nope. Now, we're getting to scorched-earth-type stuff. Oh yeah. Third option is you fight back. Because either way, I'm getting my stuff. I'm a material guy living in a material world, you boogers, and I'm not leaving without my material. So, if I start shooting, and you don't give in, it's gonna be—it's gonna be bad, you guys. And that's only if it's just *me*. Because I don't know where you put my buddies, but when they get up, you're going to *wish* it was only Star-Lord knocking you around. Because we're the Guardians of the Galaxy. And no one punks us."

The Putrilines, all at once, began to trudge past Star-Lord, gripping the crates with their gooey limbs, making their way back toward the small city in which they'd poisoned the Guardians. Star-Lord, incredulous, kicked off on the spongy, green ground with his rocket-powered boots and landed in front of the group of aliens once again, blocking their path. Without missing a beat, the group redirected, moving to the left of him and walking over the spongy ground in the direction of the tavern. Star-Lord spread his arms wide, his voice an octave higher.

"Come on, you guys," he said. "Do you really want to make this a thing? We had a good time last night. Remember? I mean, it sucks that you doped us, but all things considered, those drinks were still pretty awesome. *And* you didn't take my helmet, so clearly you don't want to *kill* me . . . just horribly rob me so I can't make enough of a living to get to the next planet. Which, yeah, jerk move, but I think we can move on from this. Right?"

One of the Putrilines stepped forward, the thick gel on its body quivering with every step. It trudged up to Star-Lord, until they were face to mass-of-gunk-that-Star-Lord-assumed-was-a-face. Slowly, purposefully, it spoke, annunciating its words. Through the thick layer of muck that had made its voice difficult to hear previously, Star-Lord managed to understand two of the three words: "Go," a harsh sort of gloppy sound, and then, finally, "yourself."

"Oh," Star-Lord said, nodding. "It's like that."

Star-Lord swung his foot up and kicked the Putriline in the face while triggering his boot's rocket power, sending a burst of flame into the gelatinous alien. He shot back from the force of the rocket, but craned his head just in time to see the satisfying explosion of slime where the alien had stood a moment before.

Star-Lord flipped over and landed, not missing a beat as he strode back over to the aliens, who were now chattering loudly in a furious series of mushy noises.

"Okay, so as you can see, I just option three'd the slime out of potty mouth over there. Are we ready to make nice and go back to option one?" Star-Lord said, rolling his shoulders as he moved toward them. "I take my crates, maybe knock a few of you in the head just because you've earned it, you tell me where my buddies are, and boom—sayonara."

This time, the masses of slime didn't look at him as if he was an idiot. This time, they began to heave up and down, emitting a strange, high-pitched gasp that built and built until Star-Lord began to think his brain was going to explode. It was like a thousands cats, a thousand car alarms, and that crisp static that he used to hear when he tried to watch a TV channel he wasn't supposed to watch as a kid mixed together in a horrific symphony.

Gritting his teeth, Star-Lord prepared to boot blast another of the aliens to stop the noise, but then remembered something from the night before that had been lost in his ale-induced haze. He'd heard that sound before, albeit a far quieter and less nails-on-a-chalkboardy version. Groot, upon drinking his tenth pitcher of the planet's purple brew, had passed out with a thunderous fall that knocked Rocket off of his chair. As Star-Lord and his other companions, Gamora and Drax, laughed, the small group of Putrilines in the bar joined them, letting out that shuddering gasp.

It was a laugh.

Now, as Star-Lord watched them cracking up before him, he wondered what exactly they found hilarious—but he didn't have to wait long to find out. A Putriline the size of an Earth mouse leapt onto Star-Lord's head and began pulling at his mask. Star-Lord went to smack it off, but two more of the tiny blobs leapt from the ground and hit his face with wet slaps.

"Where did you little snots come from?" he asked, and felt another stick to the back of his head. They crawled up his neck, each of them trying to pry his mask off. "Get off! Come on! What, you guys are using your little baby slimes to commit murder for you? That's pretty dark, not gonna lie."

As he plucked the creatures off, their bodies sticking to his helmet with the consistency of the toy slime his mother used to buy for him back in what now seemed like a different life, he saw that these weren't new foes that had been hiding among the group as he'd thought. They were coming from the remains of the first alien Star-Lord had zapped. No . . .

they *were* the first alien he'd zapped, only now that he'd blown it to pieces, he'd turned *one* foul-mouthed, huge booger into a hundred foul-mouthed, tiny ones.

His frustration and disgust building, Star-Lord swiped over and over at his face, the high-pitched laugh of his enemies building so loud that it blocked out the familiar hum of the *Milano* lifting off of the ground.

The wind caught Star-Lord's jacket, kicking off a dramatic billow that put the earlier billow to shame. However, this time Star-Lord was covered in tiny aliens and being laughed at by his enemies, so the effect was admittedly dampened.

But the gust of wind was enough to get Star-Lord to look to the sky, where he saw something that made him beam from within his mask.

"Hey!" Rocket cried, leaning out the port of the *Milano*, which now floated twenty feet in the sky.

The *Milano* was a glorious ship, sleek and V-shaped. Cool blue, fiery orange, and gleaming silver, the ship—by Star-Lord's estimation—was the prettiest thing in this or any other galaxy . . . and it didn't hurt that it had the power to leave Putriline with double the holes. The ship lit up the immediate area with a harsh, blue light that glowed from its layered wings and from within the tempered-glass flight deck. It was on autopilot, hovering above them as Rocket walked across its surface pointing a gargantuan laser cannon, hoisted on his shoulder, down at the Putrilines.

"Listen up, ya lispin' wads of scum!" Rocket's voice was gruffer than anyone would expect upon meeting him, which, while he would call that out as prejudiced, made sense considering he was a four-foot-tall raccoon. His weaponry, however, more than made up for his diminutive physical presence. "Ya got three options! Option one—"

"No options!" Star-Lord called up to him. "They do not respond well to options!"

"Welp! You heard the man!" Rocket replied, keeping the cannon trained on the aliens, who looked up at him, their laughter dying. "Put down the cargo, let go of my buddy's head, and I won't fry ya! That multiplying trick might work when Star-Lord shoots you with his little booties, but I'm packin' heavy, you understand me?"

"Really, man? Booties? I'm down here with no weapons! That kick move was pretty slick!" Star-Lord yelled back.

"You're very impressive!" Rocket shouted. He pulled a lever on the laser cannon and it let out a high-pitched whine, light bursting out of its muzzle. "Last chance, grease buckets! You want to sizzle over some boxes you don't even understand, or are you gonna make like a bunch of nice little disgusting goops and give me mine?"

"We . . . have . . . nothing . . . here!" one of the aliens shouted, struggling to pronounce each word through its slimy maw. "Leave . . . your . . . goods . . . and leave . . . alive!"

"You have nothing?" Rocket asked, incredulously. "You

kidding me? You got ale, you got a . . . a tavern, some shacks. What do you need with crates?"

"We . . . are . . . not . . . dumb! We . . . know . . . what . . . this . . . is . . . worth."

Star-Lord looked up at Rocket. "And there we are."

"Yep," Rocket said, grinning. "There's my answer."

No sooner had Star-Lord heard the thunderous sound of the laser cannon than he was hit with a hot wave of slime. Disgusted as he felt the gunk sizzle into his uncovered scalp, Star-Lord wiped off the final remaining mini-Putrilines and kicked off the ground. He hurtled through the smoking field of moss as Rocket let off another blast.

Star-Lord scooped up one of the crates, which had been completely covered in slime, and lifted it off the ground. He rocketed up to the ship and tossed it in, hoping quietly that the packaging had been enough to protect the contents from the noxious gunk that had once been the Putrilines.

Before he headed back down to the ground, he stopped next to Rocket, who was laughing like a madman as he let off blast after blast.

"The others?" Star-Lord asked.

"All on board," Rocket said, pausing his volley for a moment. "Slimy freaks tied us up with some gluey crap and dumped us all over town. Should've killed us if they were gonna do that."

"I don't think they wanted to hurt us," Star-Lord said.

"Just another thing me and them don't see eye to eye on," Rocket said, hoisting his cannon.

"Hey, wait a second," Star-Lord said. "When did you guys get on the ship? I've been dealing with these guys for, like, ten minutes!"

"Yeah, we saw that," Rocket said, laughing. "Gamora said she thought you had it under control, but I figured I'd step in. It was fun to watch for a while, though."

"You're hilarious," Star-Lord said. "Really."

"It was!" Rocket said, his eyes gleaming as he popped off another shot.

"Watch out for the other crates! If you shoot the boxes, we're screwed," Star-Lord said as he dove off the ship. "Be right back with the other two."

"Take your time," Rocket said. "I'm having a blast. HAH! A blast!"

"You say that exact line every time you use that cannon," Star-Lord said, spotting the two remaining crates. They were on the ground, next to what appeared to be thousands of tiny Putrilines, all of whom were now far too small to even lift the crate. Chuckling, Star-Lord flew down and took the last of the crates one by one back to the ship.

"Hold on," he said, stopping Rocket from closing the hull. The slime that coated the boxes was beginning to reconstitute into tiny Putrilines who yelled in a high-pitched, mushy cacophony.

"Go on," Star-Lord said, swiping the balls of slime off the crates and knocking the final Putrilines back to the cavernous, mossy surface of their planet as the ship lifted higher into the air. "You're all clearly not stealing our stuff. You're like an inch tall. Get out of here."

"I'll hate myself for sayin' it, but these gross little pukes are actually pretty cute when they're little," Rocket said, sneering. "What's their deal, do they not die?"

"I guess not," Star-Lord said. "Honestly, I kinda don't blame them for trying to take our stuff. I bet that was the most interesting thing that's happened on their planet in years."

"In that case, I don't hold no grudge against 'em," Rocket said. "I've had worse mornings, I'll tell ya that. Way worse, Quill. You can't even *imagine* the type of things I've woken up—"

"Yep, you are totally right, bud," Star-Lord said. "I can't imagine it. Let's keep it that way."

As the *Milano* broke atmosphere, Star-Lord and Rocket, side by side, disappeared into the ship. Now that they'd recovered the cargo, they were nearing the end of a long journey that, if it went smoothly, would end with a payday that could have them living the good life at only the finest of resort planets for the better part of a year. Star-Lord was a firm believer in not jinxing something good by getting excited before the mission was complete, but when he closed his eyes, he saw clear skies, strong drinks, a lady friend, a pool the size of a planet, and exactly zero living snots in sight.

It was something worth hoping for, and these days, that's all Star-Lord really needed.

CHAPTER TWO

Skybound Life

Rocket

A short while later, Rocket sat at the dinner table with his friends, tuning out as Star-Lord recounted a hyperbolic version of his encounter with the Putrilines to Gamora, Drax, and Groot over that night's meal, made up of whatever scraps they had remaining in the fridge. Rocket's mind was elsewhere, busy thinking up increasingly sordid scenarios in which he'd spend his copious earnings once they cashed in on the bounty.

Rocket considered going to Drumog, a small planet comprised entirely of hot springs . . . but then remembered that at least two of his exes lived there, and they'd be none too happy to see him after how he'd left things. One of them was an expert with throwing stars, which had seemed appealing at the time, but now the thought of that just made Rocket hold his bushy tail close.

Dismissing that idea, his mind drifted to Baltagor, a planet of hyperintelligent reptilians that had turned almost every available surface into a gambler's paradise. Casinos, cage-fighting arenas, monster-truck pits—even the thought made Rocket rub his little paws together greedily. He thought of all the ways he could spend and make money there, and began formulating a plan to convince Groot to sign up for cage fighting when he noticed that Gamora was staring at him with a single eyebrow raised and a dull, disapproving stare— an expression that Rocket knew well.

"Were you just rubbing your little paws together?" Gamora asked, a smirk spreading across her face. Even when she was lightly taunting her friends, she exuded power and confidence. She was tall—by Rocket's standards especially—with jade-green skin, black hair that turned purple near the tips, and green eyes. The definition of a warrior, she was confident, calculating, and, as Rocket would say, *ripped*.

Rocket returned her smile and snickered. "Yeah, yeah. Concocting an evil plan over here. Let a guy be."

Rocket and Gamora shared a special bond. They were both the last of their species—utterly unique and utterly alone. Rocket didn't like to talk much about his past, especially while sober, but he deeply empathized with Gamora. Not only was she the sole surviving Zen-Whoberian, she was also the adopted daughter of interstellar tyrant (and complete douche) Thanos, who had once tasked Gamora with carrying out some rather unsavory tasks for his wicked purposes. Instead, she turned on Big Purp (Rocket's pet name for the gargantuan, violet fascist) and joined up with the Guardians of the Galaxy, with whom she now carried out unsavory tasks for money . . . and to save the universe.

Totally different.

That shared bond was what Rocket liked best about being a Guardian, though. Saving lives was all well and good, and the money, well, he couldn't lie . . . it was a sweet gig when they struck gold. But when Rocket looked around that table at his only friends in the universe, he knew that they might all be alone in some ways, but at least they were alone together.

Drax—Drax the Destroyer, governmentally—was a hulking mass of muscle, but as Rocket watched him choking on his water after laughing mid-drink at Star-Lord's impression of the Putrilines' voices, it was easy to forget that Drax could crush a skull with the effort it took someone else to twist off a bottle cap. His past was colorful as Gamora's, and similarly linked to Thanos: Drax's entire family had been murdered by an assassin working for the mad tyrant. Drax emerged from the loss as a warrior, intent on hunting Thanos down and avenging his family's lives, but the Destroyer found that vengeance, as lucrative a business as it was, was beginning to drive him mad. Thus, he joined the Guardians and began to channel his rage into something constructive, but still, when the time came, destructive.

"I am Groot," Groot bellowed, getting up from the table. Groot was Rocket's best friend in the entire universe, and it wasn't just because Rocket could comfortably perch in his branches—Groot was kind, empathetic, and funny as hell. Groot had originally, like almost everyone Rocket considered a friend, lived on the other side of the law. Even so, the formerly criminal, currently mostly-not-criminal-except-when-the-situation-called-for-it Groot was the best person Rocket knew.

"I'm about to hit the sack too, bud," Rocket said, leaning back in his chair. While the others had been around the big lug long enough to understand his tone at times, Rocket remained the only member of the crew who could understand Groot's language. Apparently, when Groot spoke, all the others heard was "I am Groot." Rocket was aware that Groot's species, the *Flora colossus,* had stiff vocal chords, limiting the variety in their speech patterns, but still, he thought his big buddy Groot spoke pretty clearly considering.

"I am Groot," Groot called back over his barky shoulder.

"Gross, man," Rocket said, holding his nose as he scurried out of his chair. "Gangway, the walking forest just crop-dusted us."

"You know, when I first met Groot, I thought he was majestic," Star-Lord said. "Now, I'm sitting here at the dinner table, smelling his tree farts. Life is weird."

"Life ain't weird. *We* are, and proud of it," Rocket said, patting Star-Lord on the shoulder. "G'night, Quill. Gamora, Drax—I'll see all of you soon-to-be-rich bastards in the morning."

Rocket padded out of the room, wondering what it had been like for Star-Lord *before* life had gotten "weird." For Rocket, life had always been like this. Six-foot-tall snots, sentient trees, green guys and gals—that was the epitome of the norm. Not for Star-Lord, though. Before he'd taken on that name, he was Peter Quill, a human boy on the planet Earth where, as far as Rocket understood, a good number of people didn't even believe that there was life off their planet. Speciesism at its finest.

Quill grew up in the stars, though, and Earth was far behind him, but Rocket sometimes envied the fact that, far away, there was a place his buddy could settle down and call home. He was the only one of them who had that, and yet he still chose to be up here, cruising the galaxy, living the sky-bound life.

Rocket wasn't sure if he understood it, but he didn't have to. Star-Lord, no matter where he came from, was one of them.

Rocket hopped into his bunk. As soon as he hit the hard mattress, the deep, rhythmic bellows of Groot snoring in the bunk above him began to lull him to sleep. If all went well, he would wake up just around the time they'd land on Bojai, where those sweet, sweet stacks of cash were waiting. If that wasn't enough to ensure Rocket pleasant dreams, nothing was.

* * *

Rocket woke up as he slammed into the floor. Before he could right himself, or even gather his thoughts, something heavy and wooden fell on top of him, pinning him to the floor of the ship's bedroom. He felt Groot's weight push him down as the ship jerked to the side and then tilted harshly to the other side, as if caught in some intense galactic turbulence.

"I am Groot!" his friend cried as the two of them slid across the floor together. Rocket weaseled his way out from under Groot's massive body and grabbed one of his branches, pulling himself up.

"Don't worry about me," Rocket said. "I'm fine. Just maybe a few hundred broken bones, no big deal. What's going on? Are we under attack?"

"I am Groot!"

"Yeah, I am holding on! Let's get out there!" Rocket replied.

Groot reached out an arm and grabbed the bunk bed. He lifted himself up, using the railing to balance. Perched on his shoulder, holding on tight, Rocket watched as all of their belongings skidded across the floor as the ship jerked again. He didn't know what was going on, but he knew that he'd woken up to a far less ideal situation than he'd anticipated.

With Groot pressing himself against the wall of the ship's hall as they moved, they made their way out of the sleeping quarters. As they moved, bracing themselves as the ship jerked once again, they passed the other rooms and saw that Drax, Gamora, and Star-Lord were all already out of their bunks and gone. Groot reached out and grabbed the ladder that led up to the flight deck.

By the time the two of them made the short climb to the top, the jerking had stopped. Gamora and Star-Lord were already there, standing on the flight deck with their backs to Rocket as they looked with confusion at the touch screen before them. There were two red leather chairs—one of which Rocket liked to think of as his own, considering how often he piloted the ship (though Star-Lord, who was basically in love with the ship, might disagree)—positioned before the tempered-glass nose of the ship and the glowing gears that illuminated the desk with a nightclubesque glow.

"What was that?" Rocket asked. "Groot almost crushed me! And where is Drax?"

"Here!" Drax called from below. Seconds later, he scaled the ladder and emerged onto the flight deck, holding a neuro-blast rifle in each hand. Strapped across his body were two more plasma launchers. "I made it to the weaponry, so that we are armed in case our attackers attempt to board. Who dares assault our ship?"

"Calm down, Drax. We're not so much under siege as we are under . . . er, confusion," Star-Lord said, pointing ahead. Through the tempered glass, they saw a sight they'd seen countless times before: a black sky dotted with stars.

"And?" Rocket said.

"Take a look at the map," Gamora said, tapping out a

sequence on the touch pad. The glass came alive with blue lines that formed into an image of three planets and a blazing, blue sun. She pointed to the smallest planet, which looked almost like a moon in its size and paleness. "That is Spiralite." Of the three planets, it was closest to them, just a thirty-minute flight away. She moved her finger across the screen to a big planet with multiple rotating, iridescent rings, which was closer to the sun but still quite accessible from Spiralite. "Incarnadine." And then she zoomed in, between Spiralite and Incarnadine but much closer to the latter, to focus on the third planet. It was lush and green, but so small it looked like it should be a moon. "And our destination: Bojai."

Groot gestured to the map. "I am Groot?"

Rocket said, "He's asking—"

"Why don't we just follow the map, right?" Star-Lord asked. "Well, we did. We should be looking at these planets right in front of us, but instead . . . boom."

"Boom?" Drax said. "What is 'boom'?"

"Boom is what happens when we try to fly the *Milano* past this," Star-Lord said, waving at the empty space in front of them. "It looks like open travel, but there's something blocking us."

"Both visually and physically," Gamora added. "It's a good thing the system dropped off light speed as we neared the solar system. If it had been up for a few more minutes, we'd have hit this thing and . . . well, you know."

"This thing?" Rocket asked.

"It's solid space," Star-Lord said. "Literally. Like, space, but solid."

"Right, genius, I get the play on words," Rocket said. "But that doesn't mean anything. Space can't be solid no more than . . . uh . . . I can't think of a comparison, but it ain't possible!"

"Well, I don't know what to tell you, man. I tried to push through a few times, but it keeps shaking the ship up and pushing us farther back. There's some kind of weird feedback going on here," Star-Lord said.

"Perhaps these planets were destroyed," Drax said. "Planets are destroyed every day. I've heard tell of energy bombs that have made entire solar systems uninhabitable. Perhaps the pushback is that leftover energy."

"Nah, we'd have known if someone torched the planets," Rocket said. "The maps would've updated. When did we last hear from Bojai?"

"When they first contacted us about this gig," Star-Lord said. "It came through a third-party network, but it's legit. A month ago, Bojai was right in front of us, next to its two neighbors, sending out signals to folks looking to make money. So, what, they just blink out of existence? I don't know, but I know what I'm seeing. A whole lot of nothing."

"We would've heard," Rocket said. "Incarnadine, that's a big rock. I've heard of those people before. Seen one back on Dumlorx once, I think. Skin like a rainbow. Cute girl, good times."

"Stick to the point, little man," Gamora said.

"Point is," Rocket said, "three planets just don't go 'poof' without folks hearing. Nova Corps would be out here, checking to see who did the thing. Nah. Our money is still out there. I know it."

"You sound like you have a theory," Gamora said.

"Eh, not a theory," Rocket said, turning away from them. "I've seen something like this before, though. Techie crap. I'm gonna go out there, take a look myself."

"You sure that's a good idea?" Star-Lord asked.

"I am Groot," Groot bellowed, shaking his head back and forth.

"I'll be fine, you grandmas," Rocket said. "We've faced worse than a travel block."

"Assuming that's what it is" Gamora said.

"Yeah, I'll go ahead and assume, then," Rocket said. "The alternative is that a planet full of our money is gone, and I don't accept that!"

As Rocket climbed down the ladder and walked down to get to the space-suit storage, he laughed to himself as he heard Drax, his tone light and perplexed, say, "Quill . . . Groot . . . how exactly is it that you are *grandmothers*? It defies both gender and age."

"Metaphor again, dude," Star-Lord said.

"Ah. Of course," Drax said. "I'm getting better at this."

"You're really not!" Rocket called back to them as he picked out the smallest space suit of the bunch. He climbed into it, turned on the oxygen, and prepared to test his theory about the force field blocking their progress. He didn't know if he was right in his thinking yet, but he was sure about one thing: nothing would stand in the way of his payday.

Rocket, his head encased in a thick bulb and his body protected by a lightweight space suit, stood on the nose of the *Milano* facing what looked to be the path in front of them, void of the three planets and their sun that should, by all accounts, be there.

With him, Rocket had brought three objects:

A rock
A twig plucked from Groot
A ray gun

Rocket was best known for what he did with his weapons *after* he conceived of them, but he was nevertheless a prodigious inventor. In this situation, he'd test his theory the same way that he tested his creations. Trial, error, and observation.

First, he plucked the rock from his pocket. Holding it in his palm, he eyed the space before him through squinted eyes. He extended his arm until his paw reached past the end of the ship, and then flicked the rock at the space.

The rock drifted from his paw, gliding toward what Star-

Lord had referred to as "solid space." Rocket prepared to duck if the stone shot back at him, rejected by whatever had pushed the *Milano* away so roughly. Instead, the rock disappeared as if suddenly swallowed by space itself.

Nodding along, Rocket then pulled out the twig and did the same: reached, flicked, watched. This time, the twig drifted only for a moment, and then hit an unseen physical barrier. The force of impact should have been minor, but instead it sent the twig jerking back awkwardly, as if it had been hit by a force from multiple angles.

"Yep," Rocket said aloud. "I'm a genius."

He then pulled out his ray gun for the last part of the test. Knowing that the beam from the gun would very likely ricochet back, given what he'd hypothesized about the so-called solid space, he angled it away from the ship, taking into account the way that Groot's twig had vibrated off in an odd direction. He set the gun to stun and fired.

A neon-pink ray cut through the sky and, before Rocket could see if it ricocheted or not, hundreds of red beams were pointed at him and the *Milano* from all directions.

"MOVE AND YOU WILL BE OBLITERATED, YOUNG RODENT," many disembodied voices spoke at once through Rocket's comm device. "STATE YOUR BUSINESS."

Star-Lord's voice came through Rocket's comm device as well, hurried and panicked. "What's going on out there, man? Do you see where that's coming from?"

"First of all," Rocket said, looking up, scanning the sky for any sign of the speaker, "I'm not a rodent. Second, I'm not that young! Third, you can kiss my—"

"Excuse us!" Gamora's voice shouted over the comm, drowning out Rocket's words. "We are the Guardians of the Galaxy. My name is Gamora, and my companions are Rocket, Groot, Drax, and Star-Lord. We are making a Nova-approved delivery from the planet Glarbitz to a planet in your solar system: Bojai. I assume that I'm talking to someone from one of the three nearby planets?"

"Yeah, they've got an energy blocker!" Rocket shouted back. "Just like I thought. Those planets are all still right there, but nothing living or energy powered can go through. High-tech stuff, but nothing we can't break through."

"YOU ARE SUGGESTING THAT YOUR INTENT IS TO BREAK THROUGH OUR SYSTEM'S SECURITY?" the voices said, rising again with a buzzing echo.

"No!" Star-Lord's voice boomed out of the *Milano*. "Sorry. Listen. Rocket just doesn't really like being called a rodent. There's really no hard feelings. If you guys check with the Nova Corps, you'll see—we're okay to pass through."

"CLEARANCE DENIED. RETURN TO GLARBITZ OR YOUR SHIP WILL BE IMPOUNDED."

Rocket snarled.

"Oh yeah? Impound this!" He held out his blaster and squeezed the trigger, sending a pink beam at the space wall.

"Rocket!" Star-Lord shouted over the ship's speakers. "Groot, get out there and grab that little idiot! He's gonna get us shot at before we even see who we're talking to. Listen, disembodied voices—like I said, check with Nova. We're all good."

"IMPOUNDING IN THREE."

"Seriously?" Star-Lord said.

"TWO."

Rocket continued firing ray after ray, all of which bounced back, lighting up the sky with pink. He knew he'd probably be shot, but at this point, he was so furious that he couldn't stop himself. It didn't help that there was nothing really to shoot at.

"ONE."

With incredible speed, all of the red laser points shining down on the *Milano* from the empty sky above converged on the nose of the ship into one red dot where Rocket stood. He dove out of the way as something shot from the center of the sky and landed hard on the ship, drilling into its surface. It was about a foot tall and circular, with four metallic legs and a single red eye.

"Knew it," Rocket said. "They're drones! They're using drones to create a force field that—"

Rocket felt the air burst from his lungs as a second drone slammed into him, latching onto his chest. He wrestled with it for a moment, but before he could position his ray gun at its bulbous body, the drone squeezed him three times in rapid succession with crushing strength, causing Rocket to go limp. As he lay prostrate on the *Milano*, the drone attached to him, he watched as his gun drifted through space.

"Rocket?" Star-Lord called over Rocket's personal comm device, but he couldn't respond, nor did he have the time to catch his breath. The drones were now whirring, lifting Rocket and the *Milano* in different directions. Cracking into action, the drones whisked them through the invisible divide and into the hidden solar system that laid beyond the veil.

CHAPTER THREE

Beyond the Veil

Gamora

If I were to toss the guard into the furnace, I wonder if that would spark a riot, Gamora thought as she surveyed the over-crowded prison yard.

She was being pushed by a seven-foot-tall being down a rocky path on Spiralite, where the drones had taken the Guardians and docked the *Milano*. The same creatures ushered Rocket, Drax, Groot, and Star-Lord along in front of Gamora, forcing them to walk past a large, mixed group of aliens. Gamora recognized some of the races; others she didn't. But she could see they were all prisoners—with glowing cuffs around their ankles and wrists—and were being forced by the tall creatures to do manual labor. Most were using long shovels to dig heaps of soil from a deep pit, exposing bursts of blue flames that shot out of the ground. Some of the prisoners, their skin glistening with sweat and their gazes distant, looked as if they were about to keel over.

Indeed, as they passed, Gamora could feel the heat even from yards away. Whatever that blue flame was, it was potent.

She glanced over her shoulder, assessing the towering alien walking behind her and wondering if she'd be able to best him with her wrists cuffed behind her back, as they currently were. But even if she managed to wrestle the creature into the furnace, and in the wild scenario that her rebellion stirred the prisoners to riot, the ship was still impounded with that precious cargo, and she and her crew were facing a situation they knew very little about. Besides, beyond the prison yard, there was a large facility that Gamora suspected was the prison itself . . . which she was sure was packed with more of these silent alien guards.

As frustrating as it was, she knew that the only move was to wait it out.

The aliens were tall and thin with spindly limbs covered in a slick, black exoskeleton. Purple veins ran up their arms and ribs, and, when they breathed, their large, pyramid-shaped heads split open for a moment to reveal an expanding and contracting translucent sac. Gamora had never seen this species before, but her time working as an assassin for Thanos and subsequent years fighting on both sides of the law had trained her to notice vulnerability—and she knew, from the way the creatures' heads closed over their air-sacs when they exhaled, that was the place to strike if it came to it.

The creatures had incredible reach, though, with long arms that bent deeply at the elbow, like spider legs, and three fingers on each hand that were as long as her forearms. They hadn't spoken aloud, but ever since the *Milano* had docked and the guards swarmed in, disarming the Guardians and binding them with the energy cuffs that currently held their arms behind their backs, Gamora had heard a constant, distant chattering in the back of her head, like music to which she couldn't trace the source.

She suspected that these creatures were telepathic.

"Where are you taking us, large insect?" Drax said. "My patience wears thin."

"Your *patience* wears thin? We're in cuffs! We're passing a prison! We're past patience, my friend. We're in the middle of bust-some-heads territory!" Rocket snapped.

"No," Gamora said, keeping her tone even as the guard pushed her from behind. "We do what they say. For now."

"I am Groot," Groot said from the front of the group.

"You hear that? Groot agrees with me," Rocket said.

"Maybe let's not talk openly about our plans in front of our captors. What do you guys think about that?" Star-Lord asked.

"These shills don't speak ours or any other language," Rocket said. "Ain't that right, bug breath?"

There was no response, but the distant psychic buzzing continued uninterrupted.

As they passed the prison, Star-Lord glanced over his shoulder. It was quick, just a flash of his blue eyes, but she knew exactly what he was asking. *What's the move here?*

She looked ahead, staring placidly as if nothing at all was wrong. Star-Lord seemed to take solace in this, and he turned around, continuing to move with the group. The truth was, Gamora knew that if Peter Quill was alone in this situation, he would've already attempted exactly what Rocket had threatened to do. For much of the time she had known him, Star-Lord had been the type of man to throw himself into a situation, freestyle his way out of it, and hope that he didn't get hit in the subsequent hail of gunfire. He was impulsive, reckless, and absolutely brilliant when a situation went from bad to worse. There was no one Gamora would rather have by her side when trouble showed up, as it so often did, but Star-Lord was beginning to learn an important lesson from Gamora's cues—perhaps the only thing of value she'd learned from her father: even the most powerful person in the universe should avoid trouble if he or she can.

They advanced toward a tall, ivory building that looked like an Asgardian palace when compared to the crude stone of the prison. Gamora hadn't gotten to observe much of the lay of the land, but as the drones brought the *Milano* in for impound, she had noticed a few populated cities that they passed over, but they were spread far apart. Now here, in this area, the only visible buildings were the prison, the building they approached, and a tower in the distance, about half a mile from them, that shot bolts of blue flames into the sky. The grass was green and there were small lakes all around, so the area was definitely livable, but it didn't seem that there were any homes around.

As they crossed the threshold of the ivory building, the creature gave Gamora one last push. She turned around, tempted for a moment to aim a kick right at its air-sac, just to see if it popped like a balloon, but she gritted her teeth, fighting the impulse. Clearly, they weren't going to prison—yet. That was a win in her book, no matter how minor.

As they stood in an empty hall, sterile and white, the lanky aliens backed away from the Guardians, who stood together, looking around in confusion.

"Well?" Rocket snapped.

Gamora's head was then filled with a powerful thought. It almost seemed like a voice, but it was beyond something that she heard, and felt closer to the way she experienced her personal thoughts. It was as if, for a single sentence, her inner monologue had been hijacked. From the way her friends winced, she knew they'd "heard" the same thing: *Select a representative.*

"It spoke as me, to my brain!" Drax shouted. "This is unacceptable!"

"Hey," Star-Lord said. "Take it easy, big guy. Hold that aggression off just a little longer. Cool?"

"*Not* 'cool,'" Drax said. "I feel heat building in my body as my rage mounts. I could not be less cool!"

"True facts," Rocket said under his breath.

"I am Groot?"

"I guess we have to do what they say, right?" Rocket said, looking from Groot to Gamora. "That's what people keep telling me, for whatever stupid reason. Because if I got my pick, my representative is a knee straight to their—"

"I am Groot," Groot said firmly, shaking his leafy head.

Rocket sighed. "Fine. We'll keep playing along. If these windbags end up cooking that representative for dinner, don't forget I told ya so. Pick whoever you want."

"Gamora," Star-Lord said. "Er, not that I want you to get eaten. I'm thinking this isn't a dinner-date type situation. And if it is, if anyone survives . . . it's gotta be you."

"Thanks," Gamora said, her brows raised.

"I pick . . ." Drax said, inclining his head, deep in thought. He then closed his eyes and breathed out heavily, nodding his head in reverence. "Drax the Destroyer."

"I am Groot," Groot offered.

"That's two for Gamora," Rocket said. "Fine. Peace wins out. Gamora, go talk them to death so we can get our *ship* out of here and make some *money*! I swear, if we lose this job, we're coming back with some grand-scale bug spray. You understand me?"

Gamora nodded at her friends. "I'll give them your best." Then she leaned close to Rocket and, with a smile on her face, whispered, "And if they try me . . . I'll give them my worst."

* * *

34

As two of the alien guards led Gamora down the brightly illuminated, winding hall, she noticed that there seemed to be no sources for the light. It emanated from behind the walls, underneath the floors, and even from the ceiling, as if the building itself was charged with energy. Now that she had separated from her team, she noticed that her captors were no longer pushing her along as they had when they passed the prisoners and that shimmering blue furnace. Their militaristic air had eased—Gamora could tell from the way their shoulders were angled down now, rather than raised with arms locked at the elbows, ready to lash out should the Guardians retaliate.

They underestimated Gamora. She would remember that.

The hall ramped up into a wide staircase and Gamora noticed dozens of the creatures lining the halls, each of them armed with a simple energy pistol that, like the furnace and the far-off tower, glowed a bright, cool blue. They breathed in a cacophony of gasps, their air-sacs expanding and contracting, their facial exoskeletons opening and shutting with scratchy, dry smacks.

Rocket's joke about the creatures feasting on her suddenly sounded less ridiculous.

Once the original two guards led her to the end of the hallway, the group of aliens parted to reveal an ornate set of double doors, white as the rest of the buildings, but carved with a series of symbols that Gamora didn't recognize. The symbols lit up in a sequence: top left, bottom right, center. She concentrated on the doors, attempting to store a mental image of the symbols in order to have something—anything—against these creatures if it came down to a battle. Based on sheer numbers, she knew she and the Guardians wouldn't stand a chance in a fight at the moment, but with information, time, a plan, and enough piss and vinegar, Gamora would never bet against her team.

Before she could commit the full set of symbols to memory, the doors opened outward to a room that was alive with color. A deep, plush, purple carpet, blue walls so dark that they were almost as black as a starless sky, crude red and orange paintings that were hung all over the walls along with framed certificates and plaques that looked like awards. After getting accustomed to the sterile, white building, it was an assault on the senses, causing Gamora to blink her eyes hard as she was pushed into the room.

The doors shut behind her.

She opened and shut her eyes a few more times before she was able to take full stock of the room. There were none of the looming aliens, but neither was she alone. In the far corner of the room, on the other side of a black desk that blended in with the wall, sat a humanoid creature—in fact, for a moment, Gamora mistook the alien for an elderly human male. His eyes were concentrating on the surface of his desk, which shone with a series of digital images. Using a delicate, webbed, four-fingered hand, the alien swiped a few of the projections aside and then, with a deep sigh, looked up at Gamora.

"Hello, there," he said. His nose, almost flat against his doughy face, led into his lips, which parted over a series of small but dull fangs, somewhat like an Earth cat. With light-pink flesh and big eyes that were pools of deep blue, no irises or whites, the alien seemed far less outwardly aggressive than the guards. But Gamora's journeys had taught her that sometimes the seemingly innocuous beings were worse than the giant hissing monsters with razors for teeth, so she wasn't prepared to let down her guard quite yet. Physiognomy was for the weak minded, and Gamora had never counted herself among that crowd.

"Hello," Gamora said. She noted that the creature was fully clothed while the insectoids had worn nothing. This alien was covered up to his neck in a formal garment, pure white except for a glowing blue pin over his right breast pocket.

"I am Emperor Z'Drut of Spiralite," he said. "You are Gamora, daughter of Thanos."

"Which is not my preferred distinction," she said.

"Guardian of the Galaxy," Z'Drut said, smiling widely, his cheeks plushy and his eyes bright.

"That's right," Gamora said.

"It's nice to meet you," Z'Drut said. "I don't believe Spiralite has ever had the pleasure of welcoming a Guardian of the Galaxy . . . as helpful as that may have been for us, in our trying times."

Gamora narrowed her eyes at Z'Drut, assessing him as he smiled at her. His words might have sounded passive aggressive coming from someone else, but there was something about his measured tone that sounded truthful.

"While it's nice to meet you, Emperor Z'Drut, I must say," Gamora said, "if you know who we are, then I'm confused as to why you're keeping us from our destination."

"Hm," Z'Drut said, touching his chin with a finger. He closed his eyes, seemingly mulling over Gamora's words, and then looked back up at her. "Please, please. Sit."

Gamora walked over to his desk, in front of which was a short, flat stool with no back. The handcuffs made lowering herself onto the seat difficult, but she did her best, bending her knees, careful not to fall backward. Z'Drut watched her awkwardly plop onto the stool. It must have been designed for someone much taller—likely, one of the alien guards—as it made her look up at Z'Drut in his raised position at his desk.

"Apologies. I understand that your handcuffs make it rather difficult to maneuver," he said. "As a Guardian of the Galaxy, though, I am sure you have the experience with which to understand why I must take the precaution."

"Like I said, with all due respect, I'm not quite sure that I *do* understand," she replied. "We're not keeping any secrets. In fact, we're expected on Bojai before your sun falls. If you want to check with the officials on that planet, they'll back me up. This is a sanctioned delivery. I know that Bojai's government tends to operate in a solitary capacity, but I have to assume you aren't enemies."

"No," Z'Drut said. "Of course not. I've met with their council on multiple occasions. They are a personable, if unique, people."

"It would be easy for you to clear this, then?" Gamora asked.

Z'Drut nodded, as if she had said something with which he entirely agreed. "Are you a mother?" he asked.

"What?"

"Are you a mother? Do you have children?"

"I don't see how that's any of your business," Gamora said, her gaze darkening.

"Oh—oh, of course. It's not," Z'Drut said, smiling softly and holding up his webbed hands. "Prying is not my intention. I'm merely attempting to illustrate my unique circumstances here. Say, just for the sake of conversation, that you are a mother. You are caring for a full family of sons and daughters, bright and beautiful." He looked down at Gamora, meeting her stare. "They have your eyes."

"Where is this going?"

"Your children are dear to you. Everything you love about life, everything *good* is within them. You wish to protect them from the world because you've lived a life that you'd rather they never see. There are beings out there, beings that would do them harm for no other reason than they'd *enjoy* it. You'd like to avoid that happening. Of course you would."

Gamora stared at him blankly. "Here's a tip. The next time you try to make a point, don't assume someone is maternal just because she's a woman. It makes you look like an ass."

Z'Drut's eyes widened. For a moment, Gamora thought he was going to lash out and strike her. Instead, his lips spread open as he let out a full, barking laugh. "Incredible. You may win safe passage based on likability alone!"

Gamora forced a smile. "Good to hear. That's what I was aiming for. Likability."

"You misunderstand me, though, I must say," Z'Drut said. "My point isn't your maternal instinct, but rather your instinct to protect that which you hold dear. Children, family, friends . . . your *people*. For the sake of the completion of my metaphor, allow me. If a man passed through your village, where you and your beautiful children lived . . . and if he showed you his papers, showed you that the men who govern your land have given him the go ahead . . . well, when you find him bathing in the blood of your children, the blood of those sweet little babes that had your eyes, that were so good, so pure—do you then welcome the next visitor with open arms?"

Gamora's legs tensed. With every word Z'Drut said, she was more and more convinced that he hadn't brought her in here to talk. His tone was light, friendly, but Gamora could sense a fire behind it. She didn't know what her crew had done to get that fire directed toward them, though, but she was prepared to spring into action if he made his move.

Z'Drut stood. "Let me be clear. I don't wish to do you harm, nor do I have any ill intent for the Guardians of the Galaxy. But you must be empathetic to the struggles of my people."

"Who *are* your people?" Gamora asked. "I haven't seen any-one on the planet besides *you* and the things that brought me in here. I'm not sure if those are the people you're referring to, because they don't look or act much like you. If you're giving lessons in empathy, you might want to start with them."

"Ah, the Thandrid," Z'Drut said. "Appearances may be deceiving. As someone who travels with the ones called *Rocket* and *Groot*, you know that to be true. The Thandrid are boundlessly intelligent, deeply emotional creatures. They reached out to my people, and I was happy to broker a deal with them."

"They're not from this planet?"

"No," Z'Drut said, "though we now gladly share Spiralite with them. This city, my capital, Z'Drulite, is now considered our shared territory."

"What could have led such a careful leader to giving up part of his planet?" Gamora asked. Then, with a tight smile, she leaned forward and added, "Not to pry."

"I assume that you've done your research about this solar

system before setting your path to Bojai," Z'Drut said. "You'll know that Spiralite is known for its fuel source."

"I know a fair bit," Gamora said. "Light-based energy. Renewable. Powers machinery. Can be weaponized. Incredibly powerful."

"Indeed" Z'Drut said. "It is more than that, though, but that is not important for our purposes. What you must understand to appreciate the difficulty of my position is that, though the Nova Corps have vowed time and time again to protect my people, our precious natural resources have made Spiralite the target of invasion after invasion. The Skrulls, the Kree, the Tribbitites . . . our population has been decimated, our culture destroyed, so that these monsters could sap our planet of its energy and leave us to succumb to their attacks. And we very nearly did . . . until the Thandrid reached out to us."

"I can empathize with that," Gamora said. "I don't need a motherly metaphor to understand extinction."

"Apologies for how I may have come off," Z'Drut said. "I don't mean to undervalue your intelligence, or what you've been through—it's merely that this is a conversation I've had quite a few times, only to see what I believed to be an understanding turn into an attack."

"So the Thandrid are guarding your planet from invaders?"

"That, and more," Z'Drut said. "I offer them free use of my planet's resources, and they, in turn, offer Spiralines a chance to live without fear of decimation. With the drone wall finally in place, and person-to-person checkpoint conversations like this one, the Thandrid have helped us catch all potential threats before any Spiraline blood is shed. It's a new age."

"Drone wall," Gamora said. "That's what blocked our view of the planets."

"Nothing organic or energy powered can pass through," Z'Drut said. "It seems drastic, but half measures have led to the destruction of my people."

"You're blocking off an entire solar system from space travel," Gamora said. "Do the Incarnadinians and Bojaian council approve?"

"The necessary conversations have begun," Z'Drut said.

"And this is Nova sanctioned?" Gamora asked.

Z'Drut smiled. "I gave Nova the consideration that they gave my planet and my people. You understand, I'm sure."

"What happens if crafts need to pass through, though?" Gamora asked, unable to keep the edge from her voice. "If you've really been speaking with Bojai's council, you know what's going on on that planet. You know why they badly need access to planets beyond your system. Cutting them off at such a trying time—"

"I am not cutting them off," Z'Drut cut in, his tone forceful but not angry. "After we speak to a craft's representative, I make the call. In most cases, I allow crafts to pass through. At worst, it's an inconvenience, but it saves lives."

Gamora narrowed her eyes. "At the prison, I saw that you had a rather diverse group of inmates. Is that also just a temporary inconvenience?"

Z'Drut held her gaze as he leaned on the desk. "Not everyone who passes through my sky has good intentions, Guardians of the Galaxy or otherwise." He reached out a hand and began to tap out a sequence on his desk's touch screen. A blue, glowing map of the three nearby buildings came up, and Z'Drut tapped on the field parallel to the prison until he had a close shot on the bunker in which the *Milano* had been impounded. "I must say that I've enjoyed this conversation. I understand that you'd rather not have met me, and that I've caused you some difficulty. Nevertheless, I believe you appreciate where I'm coming from. It is a harsh universe. Those who can't figure out how to live in it perish, forgotten to time. It is tragic, but it is the way of life."

Gamora didn't have to lie. "Yes. I can appreciate that."

"Now," Z'Drut said, his finger resting on the glowing image of the *Milano*. "I have one question left before I release you, your crew, and your ship."

"I'm glad to hear that," Gamora said. "And I'm happy to answer."

"What exactly *is* it that you're transporting through my skies in crates that are impossible to scan? Because, and this is not an accusation . . ." Z'Drut trailed off, his blue, unblinking eyes trained on Gamora, "it seems that my inspectors have gotten the idea in their heads that you're smuggling a neuro-logical plague bomb. And, you must understand that I would have an *intense* objection to that."

CHAPTER FOUR

A Declaration of Self

Groot

More than anything else, Groot was an observer.

When he observed Gamora walking toward them down the same hall along which she'd disappeared twenty minutes before, this time with an alien she introduced as Emperor Z'Drut of the Spiralines, Groot observed a change in her behavior. The consistency of her demeanor—kind, quiet, yet ready to strike—had fallen, replaced with something that Groot didn't recognize from the Zen-Whoberian warrior: uncertainty.

When Z'Drut spoke, uncuffing them and shaking each of their hands with a firmer grip than Groot expected considering the emperor's comparatively diminutive size, Groot also observed a subtle change within his friends. Peter Quill and Drax noticeably relaxed upon exchanging pleasantries with Z'Drut, their rigid posture growing more casual, more confident. Groot couldn't be sure, but after the time he'd spent traveling with them, he believed that they were gratified to learn they were *taller* than the man who'd taken them captive.

Rocket, on the other hand, had taken a turn for the worse, gripping Z'Drut's hand with a bone-crushing handshake, and hissing, "Pleasure to make your acquaintance, Your Highness," through his teeth. Groot didn't have to theorize to understand that, unlike the others, Rocket took the emperor's unintimidating appearance as an insult.

Lastly, as Z'Drut explained that he was going to have his guards do a deeper scan on the Guardians' delivery crates, Groot noticed a profound sense of peace, or something akin to it, within Z'Drut. He spoke slowly, purposefully, pausing between his words, at times for long beats, as if he was calmly searching for the exact right word to match his thoughts. While everyone around Z'Drut was sizing him up, most of them in the literal sense, Z'Drut was completely at ease. No anger, no fear, no trepidation, no interest—nothing.

Groot did *not* know what to make of that.

"Come," Z'Drut said, stepping ahead of the Guardians. He folded his hands behind his back and walked through the doors that led out of the ivory building. Groot was the first to follow him. Together, they stepped into the open air. He hadn't taken the time to appreciate it as they were being hurried along to Z'Drut's fortress, but it was a beautiful day. Groot's feet rooted a few inches into the soil, touching the roots of the delicate grass that pushed its way out of the loam that Groot knew had been destroyed and reseeded time and time again. Acts of great violence had been committed against all life on this planet. It was in the very soul of even the world's smallest seed. It was something that was so easily overlooked, how trauma exists beyond what others can see; how it becomes embedded in everything, an essential part of the world's fabric.

"Hey, Emperor," Star-Lord said, stepping up to Z'Drut, who stared toward the blue, glowing furnace in the middle of the jail yard. "Your guys will be careful with our stuff, right? I don't want to make a thing of it, but our cargo is pretty valuable. If we deliver it all busted up, we're gonna have a problem on our hands."

"The Thandrid know to be cautious with the possessions of others," Z'Drut said. "They are a careful race . . . precise in thought and action."

"I am Groot," Groot said, looking to the sky. A thin, flat craft, white but for a strip of blue light circling its center, entered the atmosphere in the distance.

Z'Drut's eyes flitted to follow Groot's gaze. Then, he turned to the others. "What did the tree say?"

Rocket opened his mouth to bark out a retort, but Groot gently grabbed his muzzle with his twiggy digits, muffling the swears.

"This is not a tree," Drax said. "This is Groot. And he said 'I am Groot.'"

Groot looked down at Rocket, raising his brows. Rocket twisted out of his grip, sneering. "It's all good, it's all good,"

Rocket said. He turned to Z'Drut. "What the *tree* said, scuzz-bag, is that there's a ship about to touch down over there. What, you got more prisoners?"

"No, no," Z'Drut said with a soft laugh. "That is a Spiraline craft, piloted by Thandrid. Since establishing the drone wall, we make daily visits to our neighboring two planets, just to ensure we're not impeding any of their business." He turned to Gamora. "Like I said . . . we're not cutting them off. I hope this proves my lack of ill intentions."

"I didn't suggest you had ill intentions," Gamora said. "I just asked."

"Hey, we, uh, we did mention that we're doing business with Bojai, right?" Star-Lord said. "I mean, I think we did. And I don't know about you guys? But on a scale of one to ten, ten being highest, I'm feeling pretty damn impeded."

"I apologize," Z'Drut said, letting out a deep sigh. "Gamora has assured me that the crates aren't housing weapons of mass destruction and, once that is proven to be true, I will step aside and you can forget my name if you'd like. On the other hand, as I fully expect to part in peace, I would be more than willing to extend the offer to have your crew dine with me once your business on Bojai is concluded. Though you may not believe me after my having delayed your mission, I'm honored to have the Guardians of the Galaxy grace our planet."

As they spoke, Groot watched as the Spiraline craft began

to descend in a smooth vertical drop next to Z'Drut's fortress. It was close enough that Groot could feel the craft emitting a slight, cool breeze that he thought the others would find unnoticeable.

Gamora narrowed her eyes at Z'Drut. "Like I said, we're carrying an antidote to the virus that the Bojaians have been suffering from. Their council specifically put in the order from Glarbitz, and I'm sure they'd corroborate that. The antidote has a small dosage of the virus, yes, but even if it were to bust open, it wouldn't be harmful. It's chemically bonded to synthetic antigens that prevent it from being contagious in this form. Completely safe, completely legal."

"And completely not a bomb," Star-Lord added.

Groot watched a port on top of the now-grounded craft slide open. His shiny black eyes squinting to see the first Thandrid stepping out, Groot tilted his head to the side. *Odd*, he thought. The Thandrid was backing out, pulling something heavy out from within.

"I'm quite sure," Z'Drut said. "I guarantee you that my team, now that they're taking a deeper look, will complete their scans much more quickly than we'd be able to get back to Bojai for confirmation. Please understand that I am attempting to have you on your way as quickly as possible, and that I apologize once again for the delay. It shouldn't be more than an hour." He paused, smiling softly. "If everything checks out, of course."

Groot watched as it became clear what the Thandrid was carrying out of the craft. It was *another* Thandrid, this one limp, its deflated air-sac hanging from its head like a wet rag. Groot opened his mouth to point this out to the other Guardians, but was unnerved to see yet another pair of Thandrid emerge from the craft—one either injured or dead, one well. Finally, a fifth of the insectoids emerged, this one walking alone with a slight limp. The port closed with a swift hiss behind them, and they disappeared into Z'Drut's fortress.

Groot turned to Z'Drut. "I am Groot?"

Z'Drut turned to Rocket, offering him a taut grin. "Well?"

Rocket looked at Groot, who stared back at him, tilting his head ever slightly to the side. With a dismissive wave of his paw, Rocket said, "Don't worry about it. He just said it's a nice day."

"Ah," Z'Drut said. "Indeed."

Rocket cast a sideways glance toward Groot, who felt a sudden rush of affection for his foul-mouthed, furry friend. Not only could Rocket understand Groot's speech, he understood the *meaning*—a distinction that Groot found precious few beings understood. Rocket knew that Groot was unnerved by what he'd seen, and that it'd be best to hide that fact for now. There could very well be a simple explanation for why the Thandrid team returning from a supposedly peaceful visit to the neighboring planets had wounds that looked to Groot like

they'd been acquired in battle, but if Groot had learned anything from his constant observations, it was this: it's the rulers
who smile as they speak to you that you should fear.

CHAPTER FIVE

The Truth about Hope

Drax

With every moment the Guardians of the Galaxy remained on Spiralite, Drax found it harder and harder not to punch everyone in sight. His muscles were tense, aching to let his fists fly—preferably into Z'Drut's smug little face. As Drax watched the alien emperor, just a few yards away from him, speaking to a trio of Thandrid, he imagined what he'd do to the runt if he attempted to imprison the Guardians. Judging by Z'Drut's size, Drax pictured a single punch sending the stubby emperor skidding across the ground like a tumbleweed caught in the wind.

Drax smiled to himself and let out a grumbling chuckle.

"This is funny to you?" Rocket hissed. "Look at them over there! They've been talking forever. If these clowns planned on letting us go, we'd be gone!"

Indeed, it had been a solid twenty minutes since the Thandrid had returned from deep scanning the Guardians' cases. They had taken Emperor Z'Drut aside, and the group had been talking—well, Z'Drut spoke while the Thandrid, Drax assumed, communicated with him nonverbally—for an uncomfortably long time.

"I was picturing how far this pathetic emperor would fly if I struck him," Drax said, his eyes flashing with glee. "Perhaps a *kick* would remove him from sight altogether."

"You know, I was totally cool with cooperating with these guys at first, but I'm beginning to think Drax has a point," Star-Lord said. "Maybe it's time to start punting."

"Wait, wait, wait," Gamora said. "What could they have possibly found in our cargo that would make them want to keep us here in the first place? The meds will check out. Easy."

"Yeaaaah, maybe," Star-Lord said. "But does 'The cargo checks out' take half an hour to say?"

"You're exaggerating," Gamora said. "Trust me, I've thought about what happens if this takes a turn for the worse. Let's just remember for a second that there are five of us on a whole planet full of those Thandrid."

"Let them send their legions," Drax said. "The Guardians of the Galaxy bow to no one. If the Thandrid attack, we will reach into their clam-faces and rip their sacs out before they can lay a finger on us. With the deflated remains of their head-lungs in our hands, we will rip them down and claim victory!"

Rocket lifted a fuzzy brow. "You're a real wordsmith."

"I am Groot," Groot said, gesticulating with his branches. He pointed to the Thandrid ship that had landed a short while before, and then to Rocket.

"A fine idea," Drax said. "That craft is bound to have an array of weapons. We will board the ship, incinerate everyone that stands in our way, take back the *Milano*, and leave this hellhole."

"Yeah, not at all what he said," Rocket said. "But nice try. Groot agrees with me. Something's not right."

"Groot, is that true?" Gamora said.

Groot held out a branch, tilting it from side to side. "I am Groot."

"*Kind of*?" Rocket repeated incredulously. "What does that mean, *kind of*?"

"I am *Groot*," Groot said, pointing at the ship once again.

"Can we go back to talking about stealing the ship?" Drax said.

Star-Lord shrugged. "I'm actually not hating that idea. Good one, Groot. Let's steal the ship."

Groot sighed deeply, turning to Rocket.

"Fine. Fine, I'll tell 'em," Rocket said. He glanced toward Z'Drut, who was still speaking to the Thandrid. Rocket lowered his voice to a whisper. "Groot thinks there's some kind of conflict going on, maybe between Spiralite and Bojai. That would explain why Z'Drut's givin' us the runaround."

"What makes you think this?" Drax asked.

"Well, when we were busy talking to Emperor Shortstuff, Groot noticed a few banged up Thandrid getting dragged out of the ship," Rocket said. "Their air-sacs were hanging down, deflated and all, they were messed up a bit—battle-wound type stuff."

"I wonder what sound their head-sacs would make if I popped them," Drax said, inclining his chin. "Would it be a *bang*, like gunshot, or a *pffffffft* like a . . ." Drax stopped and then let out a loud, barking laugh.

"Right. Fart jokes aside," said Star-Lord, "though I always appreciate a solid one, let's all give due props to Drax—if Spiralite is warring with the planet we're trying to get to, that might be a thing. That would be a great reason for them to prevent us from delivering medication, huh?"

"I am Groot."

"He says he's not sure, so don't do anything crazy," Rocket said. "But I'm beginning to think that *not* acting is crazy. We're the freakin' Guardians of the Galaxy. We're just gonna let these jerks keep us waiting as long as they want? Nah. Not me. Not when that cash is on the line."

"Look," Drax said, pointing ahead to Z'Drut who, backed by the group of Thandrid, was slowly approaching. "Prepare, friends. The moment the first of the beasts takes a breath, I'll plunge my fist into its clam-face and—"

"No!" Gamora hissed, poking Drax in the chest. "No clam-faces. No sac popping. Remember, we're surrounded by a wall of cloaking drones powerful enough to hide an entire solar system."

"A small solar system," Star-Lord said.

"Don't be pedantic," Gamora said. "Let's not guarantee ourselves an early death because we can't wait five more minutes, okay?"

Drax grumbled under his breath.

"Fine," Rocket said, speaking hurriedly as the aliens approached. "But if they try to lock us up . . ."

"Then we find out," Gamora said.

"Find out what?" Star-Lord asked.

Gamora smirked. "*Bang* or *pffft.*"

A toothy smile broke out over Drax's face. "Yes. I accept this plan."

"You all seem rather . . . amused," Z'Drut said, coming to a stop in front of them. He was as calm as ever—not quite emotionless, but certainly unreadable. "I'm pleased to see that your time on Spiralite hasn't dampened your high spirits."

"I don't see why it would have," Star-Lord said. "Unless there's a problem."

Z'Drut's placid expression didn't falter. He stood, silent for a moment, and it took every ounce of self-control within Drax's being not to swing his boot up into the little chin.

Drax kept control but still stood tense, waiting for what he knew was coming. He'd known it when they first landed, that this was no casual checkpoint—something was amiss with this planet. Drax had traveled across the universe with his found family of Star-Lord, Gamora, Rocket, and Groot, and for all of the great times and adventures they'd had, they had also seen the darkest, most terrible things of which people were capable. From fallen civilizations, to genocide, to slavery, Drax had seen it all. He couldn't quite put his finger on what exactly Emperor Z'Drut and his Thandrid thugs had in mind for the Guardians, but he knew one thing for sure—it wasn't good. With Groot's thoughts about the battle-worn Thandrid in mind, Drax began to put together the shape of Z'Drut's plan. He had surely destroyed their cargo after learning the truth about what it was, and would now try to imprison—or perhaps even execute—the Guardians. Drax balled his fists, ready for the attack.

"You have my blessing to be on your way," Z'Drut said, holding out a hand toward Star-Lord. "I am terribly sorry for delaying you. Safe travels."

"What?" Drax barked, glaring at Z'Drut, who gasped as if he'd been attacked.

"Whoa! Hah!" Star-Lord said, pushing Drax to the side with one hand, and accepting Z'Drut's handshake with the other. "Sorry, Drax is just excited. We all are. Not to say that we don't dig your planet, Emperor, we just—"

"Of course," Z'Drut said, offering a curt smile. "Understood. As I said, should you have the time and the interest after you make your drop at Bojai, my offer stands—a banquet, here, in honor of the Guardians of the Galaxy."

"Thank you," Gamora said, shaking his hand as well. "I hope we can take you up on that offer. I'd love to meet some more of your people, of whom you spoke so highly. Spiralines other than yourself would be invited, too, I'm sure?"

Z'Drut blinked. "Certainly."

Finally, as Z'Drut continued on to describe the food he would have prepared for the banquet, all of which sounded uniquely unappealing to Drax, the *Milano* glided through the sky above them and landed near the Thandrid craft.

"The crates should be checked," Drax said to Rocket as Z'Drut and Star-Lord exchanged pleasantries. "I do not trust the clam-faces, *nor* the Emperor. Something is wrong."

"Yeah, we'll check 'em," Rocket said. "But maybe *we* were wrong, bud. Sometimes, people are just paranoid, I guess."

As his friends walked back to the *Milano*, Drax stared at the Thandrid, their faces opening and closing with every gasping breath. Emperor Z'Drut stood in front of them, waving goodbye to the Guardians as they began to board the ship. In the past, when he was a different man, before he'd met the Guardians of the Galaxy, before he dedicated his life to vengeance, before his family had been murdered in the name of Thanos, perhaps Drax would have hoped that he was wrong about his misgivings, that Z'Drut was merely a paranoid ruler who had made an uneasy alliance to protect his people from the dark reach of extinction— that Drax would leave this planet with his friends and that everything would go according to plan from here on out.

But hope was something that Drax had left behind a long time ago.

"Good-bye!" Emperor Z'Drut called out to him. "May you arrive safely!"

Drax called back to him. "I'll make sure we do."

He held the emperor's gaze through narrowed eyes for a prolonged moment before turning around to catch up with the others.

Star-Lord closed the port behind Drax, who scanned the cargo area. Rocket was standing on one of the crates, giving him a thumbs up. "All's good. No damage."

Drax grumbled.

"I am Groot," Groot said.

"I don't know, bud," Rocket said. "Assuming there's a war is a big leap, ain't it? At least we're getting out of here and heading toward our disgustingly rich futures."

"Perhaps," Drax said.

From across the cargo area, Gamora looked at Drax. Without words, he could tell from her quiet, thoughtful expression that, despite her exchange of pleasantries with Z'Drut and her urges to keep the peace, she, too, knew that something dark was afoot on Spiralite. Star-Lord, Rocket, and Groot had lost a lot in their lives as well, but they clung to that insubstantial, warm thing: the blissful naiveté of hope. Drax envied them, and he believed that Gamora did, too. How could someone not?

Hope was a beautiful dream, but it had been a long time since Drax had had anything but nightmares.

CHAPTER SIX

Sick in the Head

Star-Lord

As the *Milano* descended into Bojai's atmosphere, Star-Lord stood in the center of the flight deck with his hands on his hips and a grin plastered on his face. He inhaled sharply through his nose. "You smell that?"

"Wasn't me," Rocket said, cranking the gear that slowed them down for final descent.

"What? No," Star-Lord said, waving him off. "*Money*. I can smell it from here. Stacks and bundles, you guys. Stacks and bundles."

"How can you possibly smell the money from here?" Drax said, shaking his head. "We're miles from the meeting point, and this ship smells of sweat, grease, and wet fur."

"I—I can't literally smell it, Drax," Star-Lord said. "Come on, man. I thought you were getting better with this."

"Drax has been in a mood ever since we left Spiralite," Rocket said. "Which is why I'm ignoring that fur comment. You get a single pass, big man. Just this once."

"I am Groot?" Groot said, patting Drax on the back.

"I don't need your comforting branches!" Drax said, standing up. "I am deep in thought."

"Really?" Star-Lord asked. When Drax shot him a look, he held up his hands, letting out a little laugh. "Sorry! No offense, dude. I didn't mean it like it sounded like I meant it."

"Not even going to try to make sense of that sentence," Gamora said.

"You guys!" Star-Lord said, looking from Gamora to Drax. "I'm sensing heavy attitude from you two. Am I wrong? Is something going on? What are you mad at me about? What did I do now?"

"Not everything's about you, Quill," Gamora said. "Drax and I share a concern about Spiralite."

"Whaaaat?" Star-Lord said, shaking his head. "Come on. I'm beyond ready to forget that place. You can't possibly be thinking about going to Z'Drut's banquet and eating his creepy food, right? Do you not remember how he described his chef's specialty as 'a gelatinous and tart creamy meat'? Because if you're into creamy meat, I can drop you off on the way to the nearest paradise planet."

"I sense that our troubles are far from concluded," Drax said. "If we return to Spiralite for a banquet, I believe that it will not be a banquet of food. It will be a banquet . . ." Drax paused, glancing from Star-Lord, to Gamora, to Groot, to Rocket, and then back to Star-Lord. " . . . of *death*."

Star-Lord snorted loudly as he attempted to stifle a laugh.

Rocket, on the other hand, didn't even try. He tossed his head back, roaring with laughter as the *Milano*'s auto-land function took over.

"Banquet of death!" Rocket hollered. "That is the best thing you have ever said, Drax."

"It's a killer band name," Star-Lord said, joining Rocket in his laughter.

"A banquet of death is no joke!" Drax barked.

"Just make sure we don't leave before the dessert of doom!" Rocket added. He and Star-Lord laughed harder, as Drax, Groot, and Gamora stood, staring at them.

"Awwww, come on," Star-Lord said, his laughter dying. "You too, Groot?"

"I am Groot."

"Guys, we made it off the planet," Star-Lord said. "They let us go. Yeah, it was a pain in the air-sac, but we're here. The Guardians of the Galaxy, hitting the mean streets of Bojai, about to collect some cold hard cash. Smooth sailing, right?"

"Sometimes," Gamora said, "I want to hit you. Very hard."

"I can understand that," Star-Lord said. "But, how about you three stop being so dour and we collect our bounty. Because if something happens? Which, hey, maybe you're right, maybe it will—we'll handle it. That's how we do."

Gamora looked at Drax and Groot, and then eased a little bit, letting out a sigh. "Fine. Agreed. We collect the bounty, but then, we don't stop. No hanging around, no drinking, no *girls*, Peter—we go. If we pass through that wall of drones without incident, I'll let my guard down. But until then, we're all business."

"All business," Star-Lord said, leading the way toward the port. "Got it. So we make the drop, get the money, and then— what was it, you said 'find the nearest pub,' right?"

Gamora said, "I swear—"

"Kidding!" Star-Lord said. "Kidding. I'm with you. One hundred percent."

He pulled the clamp to open the door, and the deep orange light of Bojai washed over them, casting a warm glow over the *Milano*. The planet's atmosphere was thick, so they hadn't seen much of the surface yet, but it was stunning up close. Vegetation stretched out before them in a wide field, lush and tall, but it wasn't the simple farmland green they'd expected from observing the planet on their maps. Now that they were close, they saw that the grass glowed with fiery light, illuminated beads of golden dew rising off of each amber blade. Star-Lord had read about this in the planet's profile—its pollen was bioluminescent, allowing much of the planet to use 100 percent natural lighting even though its larger neighbor, Incarnadine, locked in orbit between Bojai and the system's star, blocked most of it from the sun.

It was so beautiful that Star-Lord almost forgot the reason he was there—that a portion of the populace was suffering from a neurological plague that no known medicine in their world could treat. Even still, Star-Lord felt that this place was far different from Spiralite, in all of the best ways. He hoped that, at least, would set his friends at ease.

And if not that, maybe the payment would.

"Come on," he said, stepping onto the field. "Let's go make a stupid amount of money."

Things were going well on Bojai until the six-mouthed dogs attacked.

It wasn't just the bioluminescent vegetation that made Bojai a beautiful planet. Unlike the relatively bare Spiralite, Bojai was teeming with life forms, from the sentient Bojaians, the planet's dominant race, to many forms of wildlife. The various species lived together in a vegetative metropolis not far from where the Guardians had landed the *Milano*. Spread out all over the planet were huge cities that had been, as far as Star-Lord could tell, grown organically from the planet's natural flora. Buildings and homes were made up of tall, winding trees that wove together to create baskets of wood and leaves, and thick, sturdy vines formed bridges that stretched between Bojai's cities. It was stunningly beautiful and, besides a few simple devices that reminded Star-Lord of Earth's smart phones, relatively free of the technology that was often the defining characteristic of most advanced civilizations.

The dominant species, the genderless Bojaians, were tall

and graceful, with features that reminded Star-Lord of elves from the fantasy books he used to read as a kid. Their cheekbones were high, and their brows curved into a ridge of sharp, colorful, venomous horns that might look threatening on any other species, but which, on these seven-foot androgynous beings, looked elegant. Star-Lord had only seen one Bojaian before arriving on the planet, and that was through the comm screen on the *Milano*. One of the chief physicians, Kairmi Har, had been attempting to find a ship that would transport medical supplies from Glarbitz, as the Bojaians didn't have the technology for long-distance space travel, and Glarbitz ships weren't allowed passage into Bojai's solar system because of an old treaty between Glarbitz and Incarnadine. Kairmi Har had made the situation on Bojai seem quite dire, telling Star-Lord that many of its citizens were exhibiting symptoms of sudden psychosis. It was widespread and, Kairmi believed, contagious. Glarbitz's medication, which all of the Guardians had taken as a preventive measure, was a serum to be injected into the temple. If administered properly and promptly, before deep-tissue damage to the brain was incurred, it would restore the brain to its healthy state without any memory loss.

But the Bojai that Star-Lord observed didn't seem to be in a state of crisis. Instead, its people seemed at peace in a way that was almost unnerving. None of them stopped to look at the Guardians as they moved about their day through this vegetative metropolis. He suspected that maybe it was a cultural thing, that they thought it rude to balk at strangers . . . but he was walking alongside of a bipedal raccoon, a tree with a face, a sentient bicep, and the daughter of Thanos, on a planet that didn't seem to get a lot of visitors. They at the very least deserved a few side-eyes.

Star-Lord didn't put too much thought to it, though. Odd as it was, he didn't feel any hostility coming from the inhabitants, which was a great change of pace considering the experience he'd just had with the Thandrid. He wasn't as fatalistic about their interrogation on Spiralite as Drax was, but he'd had the tar beaten out of him enough times to recognize aggression, and the Thandrid oozed it. He was glad to be off Spiralite and that much closer to meeting Kairmi Har, and their money, face to face.

As they walked through the city, Star-Lord marveled at the buildings around them made from trees that shot up into the air, tall as skyscrapers, golden lines of glowing sap lining their bark. Now that they were in a clear, open space away from the hazy grasslands, they could see Bojai stretching out before them in all of its natural glory. The city was bordered by two seemingly uninhabited lands, the field they'd arrived in and then, in the distance, an even thicker patch of grassland and forest. On either side they were bordered by cerulean pools of fresh water that went as far as the eye could see. In the distant, hazy skyline, if Star-Lord squinted, he could see the vague shapes of cityscapes, but even those seemed to be more of the same: shelter that was grown, rather than created.

"Man," Star-Lord said. "I could stay here for a while. It's awesome here."

"Yeah, it's a blast," Rocket said, staring at a passing Bojaian. "I love being looked at like I'm invisible. Really nice."

"You are incredibly small," Drax offered. "Perhaps they truly don't see you."

"Do they see this?" Rocket snarled, offering Drax an obscene gesture.

"Come on, dude, you're supposed to be navigating," Star-Lord said to Rocket, who grasped a handheld version of the *Milano*'s mapping system, programmed to lead them to Kairmi's base.

"I am navigating," Rocket said. "I'm also observing. Let a guy multitask."

"Are we getting close?" Gamora asked.

"Yep," Rocket said, pointing the device at a tall cluster of four trees wound together in the distance. "Looks like it's straight ahead now."

"I hope they're not, like, panicking that we didn't make the drop time," Star-Lord said. "It has *not* been helpful that they don't have consistent communication allowances on this planet."

"Agreed," Gamora said. "I wouldn't expect totalitarian rule from such a beautiful planet, but I suppose it's silly to judge."

"I mean, they're not *official* totalitarian, are they?" Star-Lord said. "Their profile says that their reps are elected."

"Those two ideas aren't mutually exclusive," Gamora said. "When a planet has the capability of reaching out across the universe, but limits that to allowing a doctor a single call for help? That is hostile in its passivity. Trust me. I know totalitarian rule, and this is, if not it, very close. And nothing good comes of that."

Star-Lord pondered her words as they walked on. He didn't doubt her, and had himself contemplated the unnecessary difficulties of dealing with a planet that wouldn't be able to touch base with him throughout his trip. It seemed like a major problem for no reason, but he knew that certain planets had their reasons for limiting communications with others. With Incarnadine's complicated treaties and Spiralite fighting against constant invasion, he imagined that put Bojai in an awkward place—a place that demanded it to be self-sufficient until such time, like now, that it needed some outside help.

As they got closer to the four-tree building, the density of Bojaians decreased. There were still a few walking about, but nothing like in the center of the city. It was quieter here. The sound of wind whistling through the leaves filled the empty space around them.

"How do they expect us to enter their facility?" Drax said, motioning to the structure.

Groot made a climbing motion. "I am Groot?"

"Nah, look," Star-Lord said, pointing toward the largest tree, which stood in the center. A thick vine wrapped up its trunk, curling up and around until it disappeared into a basket of vegetation up top. "I think we just walk along that."

"I'm game," Rocket said. "But the doc better be there. I'm not gonna do all this walking if office hours are over."

Star-Lord started to respond, but his words caught in his throat when he saw a dark shape leap from the shadows of one of the nearby trees and land before them. Each of the Guardians was instantly on guard, ready to attack as the creature stepped toward them.

It looked much like an Earth dog, but instead of a cold nose, hanging tongue, kind eyes, and droopy ears, it had six sets of snapping jaws that protruded in different directions all over its face. It growled, gnashing its many sets of teeth, crouching low as it faced off against the Guardians, as if ready to pounce.

Rocket whipped an electropulse shotgun the length of a baseball bat from the clamp on his back. He pointed it at the dog, which took a menacing step toward him.

"Hey hey now," Rocket said, locking his arm. "I promise, furball . . . you don't wanna do this."

"Is the creature diseased?" Drax asked. "Has this psychological plague advanced into some kind of . . . *mouth* pandemic?"

"No," Gamora said. "I saw one of these earlier. A Bojaian was feeding it roots. It seemed tame."

The creature growled, its mouths snapping at Rocket.

"Uh, I'm thinking this one's *not* tame," Star-Lord said.

"I'm telling you, snappy," Rocket said, the barrel of his gun mere inches from the creature's head. "If I were a six-yapped freak like you, staring down a gun like this, held by a guy like me . . . I'd back off. In fact, I'd turn tail and—"

Rocket hit the ground before he could finish, as another six-mouthed dog, this one twice as large as the first, tackled him. It snapped at Rocket, who brought up his shotgun and shoved it into the creature's mouth. It bucked before Rocket could fire, sending Rocket stumbling away.

"Heads up!" Star-Lord called to Gamora as the first dog jumped toward her. Star-Lord grabbed the burly creature that was attempting to bite Rocket around its barrel-like chest, and ripped it away from his friend.

Star-Lord, still holding the thrashing dog, felt a dense weight crash into his legs that sent them both sprawling. For a moment, he thought that the first dog had changed directions to ambush him, but he was alarmed to see that two new six-mouthed dogs were preparing to bite his legs.

Using all of his strength, Star-Lord shoved the bigger dog at them and kicked his legs out, activating his rocket power. He shot up into the air, narrowly avoiding getting his backside bitten off by the mouth sticking out of one of the dog's chins. Now skybound, with a better look of the scene, he saw that there were no fewer than ten of the creatures attacking his buddies. They were all holding their own (*Because that's what the hell Guardians do,* Star-Lord thought) and would have no problem taking out the threat, but that didn't make the sudden attack in broad daylight in a central city any less strange.

Star-Lord pulled one of his submachine guns from his belt and loaded it with a concussive cartridge. He knew very well that the six-mouthed canines were trying to turn him into a one-armed corpse, but still—shooting to kill at a dog was just low.

As Groot smacked the creatures with his limbs, Rocket let off energy blasts from his gun, Gamora executed stunning spinning kicks, and Drax let loose all of those devastating punches he'd so badly wanted to throw back on Spiralite, Star-Lord aimed a few well-placed shots down at the creatures. At first, despite the Guardians' attacks, the dogs fought back, but once it became clear that they were taking way more blows than they were getting mouthfuls of leg, they backed away with vicious, growling yelps. Drax delivered one final punch to the biggest one, and it lifted off of the ground and landed in the forest beyond the medical facility with a heavy thud.

"Too much, man," Star-Lord said from above, watching as the dogs ran away.

"I needed that," Drax said, beating his chest. "I pictured the small emperor on the receiving end of my blows as I attacked. It was gratifying. I am gratified!"

Star-Lord landed next to Gamora and holstered his gun. "The hell was that about, you think?"

"We've crossed into an ecotone. Wilderness and civilization seem to overlap here," Gamora said. "Not always the best idea."

"Weird," Star-Lord said, scratching the back of his head. "Everyone good?"

"Yeah, not sure I'd call it 'good.' I'm covered in slobber," Rocket said. "Completely glazed in the stuff. Filthy animals."

"Yeah, I'm not a fan either," Star-Lord said. "Let's hurry up and get our money. I'm not really feeling this place."

"It's beautiful," Gamora said, "but I agree. That was odd. And, odder still . . . we're not far from the city, and just had a scrap with these people's pets in front of a hospital. Why is *no one* coming here to see what happened? That's unnerving."

"Yeah," Rocket said, curling his lip up. "I'm unnerved. And slobber covered. Did I mention the freakin' slobber? Talk about unnerving? *That* is unnerving."

"Yeah, it's weird. Not the slobber, that's pretty standard for us. Get over it, Rocket. The people here seem kinda . . . distant, I guess?" Star-Lord said.

"To put it mildly," Gamora said.

"Zombies," Rocket said. "Planet full of zombies."

"Well, these zombies are about to pay us a sinful amount of scratch, so let's maybe not scream about how weird they are. Just cross your fingers it's the last 'unnerving' thing that happens today," Star-Lord said, stepping onto the vine. "Because, and I've never said this before, but I'm looking forward to some boring, normal, non-six-mouthed relaxation starting kind of nowish."

The Guardians of the Galaxy walked up the vine and into Kairmi Har's facility without being attacked by any more multimouthed dogs. On the way up, Rocket busied himself by theorizing aloud about how the creatures could see well enough to attack them: "Echolocation? Nah, no way. They were growlin' louder than Drax's stomach is right now. You've gotta be real quiet for that to work. How could they have— *Oh*! Maybe—stay with me—maybe they have a bunch of microscopic eyes on their tongues? Huh? Maybe?"

Kairmi's facility was even bigger than Star-Lord thought it would be. Inside, it was furnished and almost modern in its appearance with its high-tech holographic computer systems and blue lighting that reminded Star-Lord of Spiralite, a far cry from the natural beauty of its exterior. There were a few Bojaians milling around the office, going about their work with bored, empty looks on their faces, but none of them seemed interested in helping direct the Guardians where to go.

"Land of the zombies," Rocket said.

"Like I said." Gamora jabbed Star-Lord in the ribs with her elbow. "A beautiful planet does not make a happy people."

"Neither does a plague," Star-Lord said. "Jeez, what do you guys expect?"

"A 'hello,' maybe," Gamora said. "This is strange."

"You know, you all and your 'every planet that isn't normal is strange' stuff! They're supposed to be strange! We're strange to them. You guys are strange to me. Let's just *ask* someone for some help, okay?" Star-Lord said.

Gamora nodded. "Sure. Go."

Star-Lord, after scanning the Bojaians within the room, approached the most beautiful one of the group. The Bojaian's horns were iridescent, glowing purple and blue, the black eyes glinting with hints of color.

"Excuse me," Star-Lord said. "Excuse me, miss."

"Not miss," they said.

"Oh. Big whoops. Mister, then, we're looking f—"

"Not mister," they replied.

"Ahk, sorry—right. I forgot," Star-Lord said. "I'm just a little flustered. We were attacked outside by some not-so-fun creatures, and we're running a little late, we know . . . but do you think you could show us to Kairmi Har? He should be expecting us."

They didn't reply. Star-Lord looked over to his friends, but then noticed that all of the other Bojaians in the room were now staring at them with dead, emotionless eyes. Star-Lord began to worry that perhaps the plague was worse and far more widespread than it had been when Bojai had contacted them.

The Bojaian before Star-Lord tilted their head and finally spoke. "Late?"

"Yeah. I mean, I think. Right?" Star-Lord said. "Maybe we got the time situation on this place mixed up. But Kairmi is here, right?"

They nodded, and extended a long, graceful arm toward an opening in the main room that led to a small hallway. "Kairmi is here."

"All right," Star-Lord said. "Thanks." He turned to his friends, mouthing the word "yikes" as they followed him through the opening and into the hall, which was lined with dark, brown walls. At the end of the hall, there were two rooms. Both of the doors were open.

"Gotta say," Rocket said. "Folks around here? Not so helpful."

"I am Groot," Groot agreed.

"Enough! We have been detained, and we did not punch. We have been attacked, and we did not kill. Now, we have been given *vague directions*? I will not stand for this latest infraction," Drax said. He tossed back his head and bellowed, "KAIRMI HAR! WE HAVE ARRIVED, AND WILL NOW ACCEPT YOUR FINANCIAL BESTOWMENTS!"

"Take it easy, guys," Star-Lord said. "I think they might be infected."

"I was thinking the same," Gamora said. "We assumed the plague would be noticeably crippling, but perhaps this is it.

Maybe this plague makes emotionless zombies."

"Poor saps. Hey, what do you guys say, if they don't come out in ten seconds, we start chanting 'financial bestowments,' huh?" Rocket said.

Before Star-Lord could reply, a Bojaian that he indeed recognized from his screen as the physician Kairmi Har strode out of the office to the right. Their horns were pale like cryolite, and their features were even slighter than most of the Bojaians. Kairmi stood in the narrow hallway and looked at the Guardians, their brow furrowing.

"Did one of you call my name?" Kairmi asked.

"I did," Drax said. "I am Drax, the Destroyer."

"And I'm Star-Lord." Star-Lord reached out his hand for Kairmi to shake, but they didn't take it, instead staring at him blankly, but without malice.

"Drax the Destroyer and Star-Lord," Kairmi said. "I don't believe we've scheduled an appointment, have we?"

"Oh," Star-Lord said, taken aback. "I—uh, I mean, not a doctor's appointment, if that's what you . . . No. It's me. Star-Lord. You know, Guardians of the Galaxy. I'm here to drop off your medication from Glarbitz. We've docked in the field just outside of city limits, so if you could come back with us and whatever transpo you need, we can get this all settled."

"I believe there is a misunderstanding," Kairmi said. "You're saying that you have medication for *me* from—from where?"

"Oh, you gotta be kidding me," Rocket said, burying his head in his paws.

"No, hold on, wait," Star-Lord said, trying to fight the growing dread in the pit of his stomach. "It's *me*. You and I spoke. We even had a bit of a bantery thing going on. Remember, I was like 'Hey, Glarbitz has pretty awesome snack cakes, too, do you want me to bring those?' and you were all, 'He-he no, just the medication.'"

"Why would we need medication?" they asked. "This is a hospital. We have our supplies."

"That's *it*," Rocket said. "They're blowing us off because they've already cured the disease!"

"I do not accept this," Drax said. "We have done the work and now we demand financial bestowments."

"Financial bestowments! Financial bestowments!" Rocket said, pumping his fist with every syllable.

"Hey, hey, hold on, you guys," Star-Lord said. He turned to Kairmi, appealing to them. "Listen. If that's the case, if you guys cured the disease already, that's awesome. It's great. For everyone except us. We still need payment, okay? We came a long way and used a lot of supplies to get here, so I'm gonna need you to be honest with me, because I really don't want to do anything totally uncalled for to your beautiful tree-building, which I think would be super easy to burn down. The people of your world . . . they're infected, right? They're not naturally like this. They can't be."

"Sure they can!" Rocket snapped. "I've seen weirder people. Like Groot!"

"I am Groot," Groot said.

"Yeah, and like me!" Rocket yelled.

"Ignore them," Star-Lord said. "Tell us the truth, Kairmi. What's going on here?"

Kairmi cocked their head to the side. "Disease?" they said, one of their eyes twitching. "I do not know what you're talking about."

Star-Lord looked back at the others as Kairmi stood, one of their eyes twitching violently.

"Well . . . crap," Star-Lord said. "This one's not lying, you idiots. They're infested."

"Badly, it seems," Gamora said, waving a hand in front of Kairmi's face. She snapped her fingers a few times, but Kairmi stood still, no movement but the twitch of their eye. "They're broken."

"I am not broken," Kairmi said. "Everything is fine. We are fine."

"Fine, fine, fine. Okay, yeah, clearly Kairmi here is infected with the wackadoo virus," Rocket said. "I was wrong, let's not mention it, let's move on. We'll go get a crate and bring it back ourselves. All we have to do is, what, pop 'em in the head with the syringe? They heal up while we sit tight, and then we get our money. Right?"

Gamora nodded. "Maybe."

"I am Groot," Groot said, pointing to the other door. A figure now stood in the previously empty doorway, clearly a Bojaian from their height, but their natural grace was gone. Their body was bent over, shaking, gnarled.

"Hey," Star-Lord said, taking a step closer to the Bojaian. The dim light that emanated from the leaves lining the ceiling showed a haggard figure, ravaged by a disease that Kairmi Har, clearly affected themself, no longer believed existed. An oily black ooze dripped from this Bojaian's ridge of horns, and a deep, purple bruise ran from their forehead all the way down to their neck. Beyond the sick Bojaian, Star-Lord could see that the room was filled with more figures just like this one, some of them moving, some deadly still.

The Bojaian's lip trembled, as if they were struggling to speak. Holding out his hands, ready to catch the weakened alien, Star-Lord approached.

"It's okay," Star-Lord said. "I promise, I'm here to help. Let me get you to a seat, okay? We don't want you falling down."

"Ugh," Rocket said, shaking his head. "This thing is worse than I thought. You're sure we're immune, right?"

"Come on," Star-Lord said, putting his arm around the Bojaian's waist. "Let's just take a seat over here . . ."

The Bojaian held out a hand, gesturing back toward the room. "*We* . . ." they croaked, a wet and pained sound.

"I know," Star-Lord said. "We're gonna help you. We've got an antidote to whatever's hurting you."

"*We . . .*" they said. "*We . . . are not . . . us.*"

With that, the Bojaian lurched forward, their body shaking violently as they fell face first toward the floor. Star-Lord, ready for just that, caught the sickly alien before they could hit the hard wood below, holding their body as it convulsed. Star-Lord knelt down to the ground, hoping to lay the Bojaian on the floor, but then, right there in his arms, the alien fell limp. Star-Lord, his chest tightening, put his head to the Bojaian's chest to search for a heartbeat—he didn't hear anything in their chest, but admittedly, didn't know the species's biology. Another sound instantly caught his attention, though, coming from higher up—a dry, deep, ripping sound. Star-Lord looked up at the Bojaian, perplexed as he realized that the muffled tearing noise was coming from within their head.

The bruise on the Bojaian's face seemed, for a moment, to be stretching. Star-Lord narrowed his eyes in confusion and then gasped in horrified shock when the skin on the alien's face split in a fissure that followed the length of the bruise. Star-Lord felt Gamora's hand wrap around his bicep and pull him away from the Bojaian before he could even process what was happening.

The Bojaian's face split open, just like a Thandrid's, to reveal a pulsating, veiny orb where the alien's brain must have been before the infection took hold. Star-Lord's hand found the grip of his gun just as a tiny, spindly, black limb popped out of the orb. From the way the orb moved, there could have been hundreds of creatures in there, ready to rip their way out.

"What *is* that?" Rocket asked, holding his own weapon at arm's length.

The only answer came from Kairmi Har, who was facing away from them, still standing in the same place, their eye twitching as a single bead of black ooze dribbled down their brow. "Everything . . ." they said, as the egg in the dead Bojaian's head ripped open to reveal dozens of Thandrid spawn the size of tarantulas, "is fine."

CHAPTER SEVEN

A Distinct Lack of Financial Bestowments

Rocket

Rocket reeled back his foot and, with a great battle cry, launched one of the Thandrid spawn across the room with a swift kick. It smacked against the wall, its miniature face splitting open as it slid down to the floor, revealing a tiny air-sac that looked like a gum bubble. Rocket prepared another kick, but Star-Lord plucked him off the floor, allowing the Thandrid spawn to scurry past them, skittering into the hall on their tiny legs.

"Hey! Get your paws off of me, Quill!" Rocket said, writhing in Star-Lord's grasp. Below him, the spawn he'd kicked, still dazed, followed after its newborn kin, stumbling as it walked in half circles, falling every few steps. "They're getting away!"

"Come on, man," Star-Lord said, setting Rocket down. "I'm totally into the idea of those creepy little freaks *not* attacking us, so maybe let's let them run out of the room and see where they're heading."

"Yes," Drax said, walking down the hall in the direction in which the Thandrid spawn had scurried. "We will follow the tiny Thandrid. Surely their journey will lead us to answers. Also, I told you so."

"*We* told you so," Gamora said.

"Yes," Drax said. "But I told you so first."

"I am Groot," Groot corrected.

"Hey, hey—really? You guys told me so?" Star-Lord said, falling into step with Gamora and Groot as they followed Drax back into the main area of the facility. "I don't know what I missed, but I don't remember either of you calling it that Thandrid, uh, impregnated the Bojaian's *faces*, all right? I don't recall anyone mentioning that as a possibility."

"Let's dial back a second. You guys are thinkin' about *answers*?!" Rocket shouted, his fury building. "Isn't anyone concerned about our stinkin' money?"

"Yes!" Drax, Gamora, and Star-Lord said at once.

"I am Groot!" Groot added.

"Fine," Rocket said, running to the head of the group. He noted that none of the Bojaians milling about the facility seemed perturbed by the fact that a swarm of Thandrid spawn had just scampered through the room. He wondered how many of them were hosts of the Thandrid eggs, if that's what was going on. "I know you all want to be smart about this, to sit back, observe, and then make a plan—but let's not forget we need this payment or we're fresh out of supplies. And fuel. We're not leaving this planet without cashing in. We can't."

"And what exactly are you suggesting we do?" Gamora asked.

"Let's walk while we talk," Star-Lord said, holding open the door, gesturing for them to step onto the vine that descended back around the thick trunk of the center tree and down to the ground, where the Thandrid spawn were already trundling. "These things are pretty freaking fast."

"I'm suggesting . . ." Rocket trailed off, and then stomped roughly on the vine as he walked. "I don't know! We've got a planet full of folks who I bet all have eggs in their heads, right? All that cash that they don't remember promising us has to be laying around somewhere."

"I am Groot," Groot said.

"What do you mean we don't *know for sure* that's what happened?" Rocket asked. "You saw what I just saw. Our contact was basically drooling when they told us they didn't remember us, and then their patient's face opened up to reveal a Thandrid party! Is this really not clear to anyone else? Anyone?"

"What are you suggesting?" Drax asked.

"Obviously, the Thandrid are every bit as screwed up as we all knew they were," Star-Lord said. "They must have heard that Bojai was suffering from this plague, and took the opportunity to invade."

"I think it goes deeper than that, buddy boy," Rocket said, pointing at his own head. "Literally."

"I think Rocket's right," Gamora said. "What if this disease the Bojaians have been suffering from wasn't a neurological plague at all? What if they'd really been infested with—"

"Face babies," Rocket finished for her.

"Sure," Gamora said. "Not what I was going to say, but sure."

Star-Lord shook his head. "I don't know. If the Thandrid are, uh, using the Bojaians to make their face babies, then why would they clear us to come to the planet with a serum?"

"Maybe because the serum wouldn't *work*," Rocket said.

"They could've just killed us there," Star-Lord said. He jogged toward the last few curls of the vine, holding a hand above his eyes and looking around. "No dogs in sight. We're good."

"They could've tried," Drax said. "Never underestimate the rage of Drax the Destroyer. I will burn their world for their trickery, starting with the tiny king."

"Assuming that Z'Drut himself doesn't have an egg farm in his head," Gamora said.

As the Guardians made it onto the ground, the Thandrid spawn advanced into the high grasses of the thicker wilderness beyond the city limits. Rocket's mind was busy with blood-soaked fantasies about what he would do when they found where the spawn were headed. True, he didn't know the full scope of what was happening, or if they were about to walk into a perilous situation, but he'd let the others worry about that. Rocket knew four things right now, and that's all he needed:

One: he should have currently been in the process of counting a ludicrous amount of money.

Two: he was not currently in the process of counting a ludicrous amount of money.

Three: it was someone's fault—perhaps multiple someones' faults—that he was not currently in the process of counting a ludicrous amount of money.

Four: whoever was at fault had just earned themselves an appointment with all of the nastiest weapons in his arsenal.

They journeyed deeper into the wilderness, the sounds of the city in the distance falling to a blanket of silence. The glowing pollen here wasn't like it was in the field in which they'd landed—it still clung to the grass and floated in the air, but it was duller here, not as lively. With the diminished illumination, it became, with each step, increasingly hard to see.

"We're losing them!" Drax barked at the front of the group, smacking aside a tall patch of grass that whipped back around and smacked Star-Lord in the face. "I can no longer see the clam-faces through these bothersome vegetables!"

"I'd lead the way, but I'm pretty sure you just blinded me," Star-Lord said, rubbing his face.

"Amateurs," Rocket said, pushing through Groot's legs to get to the front of the group. "Freakin' amateurs, all of you. Looks like Rocket's gotta do everything, as usual."

"I am Groot," Groot grumbled.

"You're damn right I'm in a bad mood!" Rocket snapped, shooting an incensed glare over his shoulder. "And I'm gonna stay in a bad mood until I'm doing laps in a pool of money."

Rocket bent close to the ground as he walked, squinting and sniffing until he found the damp, fishy scent that the Thandrid gave off. He didn't often like to rely on this particular skill around Star-Lord, who thought it was funny to compare Rocket to an Earth raccoon—he had once showed Rocket a video of the feral beast, which Rocket thought bore little resemblance to his much more handsome self—but sometimes, a man just had to sniff his way to victory. Indeed, in just a few steps, he found the Thandrid spawn, which continued to scurry across the field, their air-sacs contracting and expanding like tiny gum bubbles as they went. Rocket desperately wanted to run up behind them and start kicking again, but he held back the impulse.

He waved for the others to follow him, and they continued through the luminescent grass and bramble. The blades were tall, reaching far over Rocket's head, but that was okay. He'd rely on the others to see beyond the immediate area. What he needed to see was sticking low to the ground. As they advanced, the grass parted before them in a well-worn path that branched off into a labyrinth of leveled vegetation. Rocket held out a paw, stopping the Guardians from advancing into the open. He peeked out from the tall grass to see, in the distance, the ground swell into a hill, under which was a deep, dark burrow. The Thandrid spawn flooded into its depths as Rocket ducked back into the grass, holding a clawed digit to his snout. He motioned Gamora, Drax, Star-Lord, and Groot to get down. When they got to their knees, gathered close around him, Rocket motioned to the burrow, and then positioned his hands as if he was holding a gigantic gun toward the hole. He jerked his body back, pantomiming a powerful shot.

Star-Lord shook his head. He pointed to the hole, and then cupped his hands into circles around his eyes, gazing exaggeratedly toward the hole.

"Is this some kind of dance?" Drax asked, his voice at full volume.

Gamora grabbed Drax, pulling him closer. "Hush," she whispered. "We don't know how powerful their hearing is."

"Their?" Drax asked.

"I kinda thought we were all on the same page here," Rocket hissed. "Remember how we were following a tiny horde of face creatures? That hole is full of those sac-brained freaks! And we're talkin' probably the full-grown variety, based on our luck."

"The clam-faces," Drax said, nodding with understanding.

"Yeeeees, the clam-faces. A whole nest of 'em, looks like! And we're gonna, what, sit back like a bunch of idiots? Wait, observe?" Rocket said, tapping Star-Lord roughly with the back of his paw. "Come on! What are we waiting for? We light 'em up, we go back into town, find some money, leave the supplies for whoever has enough of a brain left to use 'em, and we get out of here before anyone's wise to us!"

"I approve of this plan," Drax said.

"See, Drax approves," Rocket said. "What are we waiting for?"

"One, assuming that burrow *is* full of Thandrid, just remember the only thing we know: they're hatching their young out of the Bojaians. How can we be sure there aren't any innocents in that hole, kept captive?" Gamora asked. "I'm not against raining some hellfire down on them. We just can't do it blindly."

"Not to mention, we're a good trek away from the *Milano*," Star-Lord said. "We've got zero escape route, and no idea what it takes to kill those things."

"Oh, I've got what it takes," Rocket snarled.

"I am Groot," Groot offered.

"And there we have it!" Rocket said. "Groot said he'd go get the ship."

"Groot can't fly the ship!" Star-Lord snapped. "You go, Rocket!"

"I've got the big guns," Rocket snarled back at him. "It's on autopilot! All he has to do is hit a button, and it's here. He's not gonna break atmo or hit light speed. You're treating him like a tree again."

Groot nodded, frowning deeply.

"I am not treating him like a . . ." Star-Lord breathed in sharply, and then raised his hands, turning to Groot. "Okay. I'm sorry, bud. You've got this?"

"I am Groot."

"Give him ten minutes," Rocket said.

Star-Lord nodded. "I'm with it. Thanks, Groot."

"I am Groot," Groot said, as he took a lumbering step away from them, the roots on his legs growing with each stride, until he was moving so fast that he began to blur.

"All right, then," Rocket said, and before the others could stop him, aimed the cannon a few yards in front of the burrow and let off a shot. A warbling, electric-blue ball of energy burst from the four-pronged muzzle and rocketed through the tall blades of grass, incinerating everything in its way. It blasted into the base of the hill with a cracking explosion, sending clumps of glowing dirt and burnt foliage flying in all directions.

"Whoa, whoa! We just—do you not remember your own plan? We were waiting for Groot!" Star-Lord said.

"Yeah, yeah, yeah!" Rocket said, waving dismissively with the cannon. "He'll be here in no time!"

"You're crazy," Star-Lord said, grabbing the cannon away from Rocket. "You're tiny and crazy! Did anyone ever tell you that?"

"Give me that back!" Rocket said, leaping onto the cannon in Star-Lord's hands. "We might as well roast these freaks while we wait! No way they'll see us in this grass. You couldn't spot a Barglewarf in this stuff."

"I don't know what that is!" Star-Lord snapped, jerking the cannon in his direction.

"It's big!" Rocket hissed back, still holding on to the cannon.

"Get *down*, you two!" Gamora shouted. She had crouched lower to the ground, hidden by the deep grass, shielding her eyes with her hands as she gazed toward the burrow. Rocket and Star-Lord followed suit, though both still kept a vice grip on the cannon, not willing to relinquish it to the other.

A Thandrid spawn, its head titled to the side in curiosity, emerged from the burrow, looking toward the smoking crater Rocket's cannon had made in the hill. A moment later, a gleaming black claw, much larger than that of the spawn, lashed out from the burrow and pulled the miniature Thandrid back into the darkness.

"Look," Drax said, pointing a meaty finger toward the hole. "The clam-faces come."

Rocket watched from behind the charred blades of grass as a full-sized Thandrid emerged from the blackness, the glow of the surrounding flora casting a golden gleam upon its exoskeleton. Another appeared behind it, and then another.

"Give me," Rocket said, "the *cannon*."

Star-Lord glared at Rocket, and then released the weapon. "You're not the only one who wants that money, all right?" he whispered. "Do us all a favor and calm down. We need to keep our heads on our shoulders, dude."

"Yeah," Rocket said, aiming his cannon at the two Thandrid's heads. He pulled on a gear, shifting it to double-shot mode. "I'm not too worried about our heads. *Theirs*, on the other hand . . ."

Rocket waited, watching as the two Thandrid scanned the area, their faces opening and closing, exposing their air-sacs with each breath. He paced it, feeling out how long it took for each of the sacs to reach full capacity—it was a split second, but that was all Rocket needed. His claw on the trigger, his paw tensed as, for the first time, the two Thandrid faces shut at the same time.

As soon as they began to open once again, Rocket squeezed the trigger.

The blue laser-clusters shot right into both of the Thandrid's open faces, lighting up their inflated air-sacs with violent bolts of power. Both of the creatures fell to the ground, writhing in pain, before two sharp pops rang through the night and they fell still. Rocket stood to full height and saw the aliens prostrate on the ground, smoke rising from the blackened, deflated remains of their sacs.

"*Bang* wins out over *pffft*," Rocket said, holding up the cannon with pride.

Drax clapped his hands together in excitement.

"Down!" Gamora shouted, as another Thandrid emerged from the burrow. It scanned the immediate area, then crept over to its comrades' bodies. Glancing down at them, it tilted back its head and, suddenly, Rocket felt a horrific buzzing at the base of his neck. He smacked at it, and saw immediately that Star-Lord, Gamora, and Drax were doing the same, gripping their necks right under their skulls.

"What is this?" Drax groaned through gritted teeth.

"It's how they communicate," Gamora said, rolling her neck, muscling through the pain. "I suspected it back on Spiralite. They're telepathic."

"*That's* communication?" Rocket snapped. "What the hell could that have meant?"

"Uh . . ." Star-Lord said, looking ahead. "I think I know, and I kinda wish I didn't."

Rocket turned his head toward the Thandrid, and, for the first time in this whole ordeal, felt something other than anger. Fear, to Rocket, was a cowardly emotion, and he was anything but a coward. Be that as it may, while he'd never admit it, when he saw the field before them begin to crawl as

countless full-grown Thandrid stepped out of unseen bur-
rows all around them, as far as the eye could see, Rocket's skin
began to crawl and sweat prickled his brow.

"Hundreds," Drax said, and this time, his tone was hushed.
"There are hundreds of them."

"Thousands," Gamora corrected. "There are more Thandrid than we have ammunition."

"Idiot," Star-Lord said, shoving Rocket. Rocket looked
at him, wishing he could come up with a retort, but he had
nothing.

"I didn't know . . ." Rocket said, his gleaming eyes darting
all around. The Thandrid were moving, but not in a single
direction. They'd begun searching around the area, the psychic buzz building as they looked for their hidden assailant. It
felt like a static shock, but it didn't stop.

"How long has Groot been gone?" Star-Lord asked. "It's
been almost ten minutes, right?"

Rocket, Gamora, and Drax shared a look. It hadn't.

"Damn," Star-Lord said. "They're gonna find us if we just
hang out here. We have to get back to the city."

"No," Gamora said. "We stay here. If we leave our spot,
they'll see the grass moving."

"Quill is right," Drax said. "If we wait, we will be discovered."

"Then we hold our ground," Gamora said. "We fight until
Groot returns."

"I'm all for popping these freaks, but even I have to say . . ."

Rocket said, his eyes wide as he watched the Thandrid begin to advance through the grass not even thirty yards away from them, "If we throw down with them, I don't see it going well."

"Listen to me," Gamora urged. "We're not going into a fight with the Thandrid hoping to win. If they spot us, we engage. They have an army, but they're spread out across the land, and I don't see a single gun. We stay put, and we stay together, fending them off until Groot returns with the ship. Then, we leave—we regroup. Formulate a plan."

"Fine," Star-Lord said, but from his tone, Rocket could tell it was anything but. That served to further unnerve Rocket, because when Peter Quill was unsure about throwing himself into a battle, you could be sure the situation was light-years past grim. "Let's just hope they don't find us, then."

"And be prepared to attack ruthlessly when they do," Drax growled.

Together, the four flattened themselves against the ground without another word. Rocket positioned his chin on his folded arms, one paw still grasping the trigger of his laser cannon so he could watch as the Thandrid in the distance moved slowly through the shorter grass where they were. To his relief, as slight as it was, they weren't getting closer. Instead, they were gathering to the left of the group, their psychic chattering amping up as they continued to search for the assassin. The noise turned from a buzz to almost a growl, spreading heat through the back of Rocket's head. Then, oddly, Rocket felt a dollop of liquid dampen the fur on the back of his neck, but he didn't react. As the warm wetness spread, Rocket kept his eyes locked on the Thandrid, certain that they were using their telepathy in an attempt to make him act. He wouldn't fall for it.

"Rocket," Star-Lord whispered, his voice cracking with nervous urgency.

Rocket, without moving his head, glanced at Star-Lord through the side of his eyes. "What?"

"Do . . . not . . . move," Star-Lord said, his eyes wide. Next to him, Rocket could see Drax and Gamora, their expressions equally nervous, looking at something unseen behind Rocket.

Rocket couldn't help himself. He slightly craned his neck until he saw it looming over him, its many fangs gleaming as dollops of hot drool fell onto his fur. The six-mouthed dog, a vicious growl growing in its chest, gnashed its teeth as it reeled back, preparing to bite Rocket.

Rocket stifled the curse he badly wanted to let out as the creature pounced. He rolled to the side, attempting to be as quiet as possible, but he heard the thick blades of grass rustle loudly and then crisply snap as he avoided the dog's attack. Drax silently grabbed the dog from behind, attempting to shut its mouths with his arms, but he didn't have nearly the number of limbs necessary.

Four distinct howls came from the dog's open mouths, echoing through the open field. The telepathic buzz of the

Thandrid came to a sudden stop, and all was quiet in an instant. All over, in every direction, farther than any of them could see, all eyes were focused directly on them.

CHAPTER EIGHT

The Rebel Queen

Gamora

Gamora drew her blade—a two-foot-long sword, forged of a metal worth nearly as much as their collective bounty—with a musical scrape. She watched as, with long, leaping strides of their spindly, lithe legs, the Thandrid closed in on them, hissing as their faces collectively snapped shut, shielding their vulnerable air-sacs. They held up their arms, which began to shift, pulling back a layer of exoskeleton. Organic blades, covered with red mucous and serrated, slid out of their forearms.

"Annnnnd this is a thing," Star-Lord said, standing up and pulling out a plasma gun as the Guardians got into formation. Gamora held her blade low, planning her next seven moves as Rocket readied his laser cannon and Drax grasped his twin blades. They had their backs to each other, looking in every possible direction, but almost everything was blotted out by the endless swarm of black exoskeletons flooding toward them. "Stay close."

"Better plan," Gamora said. She leapt forward to meet the closest Thandrid, taking it down with her sudden weight.

Before it hit the ground, she locked her foot into its knobby hip and kicked off of it, propelling herself into the air. With a flash of her blade, she sliced up, directly through the partition in another Thandrid's face.

The blade came to a sudden stop as the Thandrid clenched its facial muscles, and then twisted. Gamora held on to her sword, but the strength of the creature tossed her into the arms of a bigger, burlier Thandrid who was ready for her. It lifted its serrated arm and prepared to swipe it across Gamora's exposed neck.

Gamora threw her legs to the ground, hard, and the blades missed her neck, but caught her bicep, which opened up in a flash of blood. Sneering, Gamora ducked low to avoid another blow and swung her blade into the back of the Thandrid's knee. As expected, it hit with a hard clink, leaving the alien undamaged.

Gamora grunted, rolling as the big Thandrid and another hissing one came at her at once. She turned, locked her arm, and charged straight at the big one. Instead of slashing her blade this time, she plunged it straight through the partition in its face, and this time, she felt the hilt tremble in her grip as the air-sac popped within the Thandrid's face.

She pulled the sword out just in time to duck down to the ground, avoiding the grasping hands of another enemy. As the alien bent, she grabbed it around the head and forced it to the ground with her. She felt the razor-sharp blades of its forearm dig into her thigh and, with a vicious battle cry, shoved the sword into its face. It was closed tightly and resisted the blade, but as Gamora forced the Thandrid's face down and the blade up, she finally felt a satisfying pop.

"Two down," she said, rising to her feet just in time to see three Thandrid closing in around her. "Seven thousand to go."

She began to slash at the trio of Thandrid, driving them back so she could get a better shot. They were all keeping their air-sacs hidden as they fought, but out of her periphery, she saw other Thandrid turn away from the battle to take a single, deep, gasping breath before returning to the offensive. As she warded the ones near her off, she watched Rocket and Star-Lord lighting the field up with laser and plasma blasts, but it wasn't enough. Thandrid were breaking through the explosions and getting close to them, leaving them to fend for themselves with punches, kicks, and pistol whips. Drax was faring better with his twin blades, the golden light of the surrounding bioluminescent vegetation gleaming off of their steel as he ran them through the Thandrid's faces.

Gamora leapt toward a Thandrid as it turned away from her to take a deep breath. She plunged her sword directly into its air-sac, which burst as easily as a balloon. The looming creature's body began to fall toward Gamora, who grabbed it by the back and, using its momentum, tossed it at the four Thandrid rushing at her from behind. It took them all down at once, and Gamora, smiling at her success, brought her blade down in four quick, brutal strikes, popping each of their exposed air-sacs.

She turned around to face the next enemy, but it was already on her. She saw the arm-blades flash before her face, and then felt a hot burst of liquid on the bridge of her nose, followed by white-hot agony. She fell back, pain shooting from her face all the way down to her toes, making her limbs lock and muscles tense. She lay there, paralyzed by the shock of the pain as the Thandrid, its arm painted with blood that Gamora knew was her own, stood over her, reeling back its arm to deliver the final blow.

Gamora, fighting her body's instinct to shut down, brought her blade up to meet the Thandrid's serrated arm. It crouched over her, pushing its arm down toward her, forcing her own to buckle. She held on to the hilt of the sword with both hands, but the Thandrid was too strong. It began to force her blade back toward her.

Gamora's vision filled with white light, blurriness bubbling up around the edges of her eye line. *No, no, no,* she thought. *Don't pass out. Not now!*

She leaned up into the blade, putting all of her strength into it, trying to force the Thandrid back, trying to get to her feet. But it was powerful, crushingly so, and Gamora was quickly losing strength. Her eyes widened in horror as she saw what she believed was another Thandrid come up behind this one, its spindly arms reaching over the other alien's shoulder for Gamora.

Gamora looked to the side, hoping to get one last look at her friends, but she couldn't see them through the endless flood of Thandrid. She looked back to the Thandrid, and afforded herself a grin. If the only real family she'd ever known couldn't be the last thing she saw, she was content to look into her killer's face and smile, showing it that, even in death, she wouldn't be broken.

However, what *was* being broken open was the Thandrid's face. The spindly limbs that had been reaching for her were not another Thandrid's arms, but instead thick, brown roots. They snaked into the Thandrid's face and into the partition, forcing it open. With two great tugs, the Thandrid's face was ripped open with a horrific crunch, and yet another root snaked into its open head and wrapped around its air-sac.

Gamora felt the gasp of foul air on her face as it popped.

The roots tossed the Thandrid aside and wrapped around Gamora's waist. Her gaze followed them up to the air above her where the *Milano* was hovering, just a few yards above.

"The light!" she said, grinning as she realized what she'd seen before.

Groot stood in the open port of the ship, his arms extended to capacity. He was lifting Gamora with one arm, and as she was brought into the sky, she saw that Groot held Drax in the other. In turn, the triumphant Drax held a still-inflated air-sac in one of his hands, which he presumably had ripped free from a Thandrid's face.

It didn't take her long to spot Star-Lord, who was ascending into the sky with his rocket-powered boots. He held Rocket at arm's length as Rocket peppered the Thandrid below with blast after blast from his laser cannon. Rocket laughed, screaming, "See ya, suckers! We'll be back for our money!"

Groot, shrinking his powerful arms back to normal length, pulled Gamora and Drax into the port. Star-Lord and Rocket landed next to them seconds later, with Rocket letting off one final blow from his cannon.

"I can hear those sacs crackling like popcorn!" he cried, his eyes shining with mad glee.

"I am Groot," Groot said to Gamora, before wrapping both arms around her in a warm hug. Gamora was taken aback, but then fell into the crook of his arms, returning his embrace. As many times as she'd been in a near-death situation, she had to admit accepting your fate was *not* something someone got used to.

"Yowtch," Star-Lord said, touching Gamora's cheek as Groot held her at arm's length. "That looks like it hurts."

Gamora breathed in sharply, wincing as she felt the cool air of the ship on her wound. "It could've been worse."

The five of them stood together, silent for a moment as the ship began to rise above the sea of hissing Thandrid below. Gamora couldn't be sure that the others shared her thought in that moment—that they were damn lucky to be standing there together, alive—but she felt a deep solidarity in that silence. For that moment, the pain was bearable, and she felt a rush of relief.

It was gone as soon as it came, though. As the port began to close and reality rushed back in, she wiped the blood off of her face and walked toward the flight deck.

"Where are we gonna go?" Rocket asked.

"That's the question," Gamora said. "Because something tells me that no matter what direction we choose, we have a fight ahead of us."

Star-Lord gingerly patted a gauze strip on the cut on Gamora's face. The generic scar-salve that they kept in the ship's cluttered infirmary was already working on the pain that cut through her nose. Her head still ached, but that was subsiding.

"All done," Star-Lord said, with a tight smile. Gamora could see it, plain on his face. He was shaken, which was natural, of course, with them just a few moments out of a battle that had been impossible to win. He knew what could've happened to her—to any of them—but it wasn't his way to talk about it. Gamora was more than fine with that.

She stood, still light headed. Without her having to ask, Star-Lord walked in step with her as she strode over to the center of the flight deck, until her legs steadied and she was sure she wouldn't stumble. Rocket was at the controls while Groot sat next to him. Drax peered out of the tempered glass as they broke Bojai's atmosphere and headed into the black. Gamora and Star-Lord came to a stop next to Drax, who looked at them with a simmering gaze.

"The tiny emperor meant to send us to our deaths," Drax said. "I will not rest until we deliver him to the reaper."

"That's one hell of an assumption," Star-Lord said.

"I tend to agree with Star-Lord on this one," Gamora said. "I don't think Z'Drut is on the up and up, but I don't see him as someone who would have to send us to another planet to ensure our deaths. He had his own army of Thandrid, all of them armed. He could've executed us there."

"Then why?" Drax asked. "You think he doesn't *know* about Bojai? He seems to be deeply allied with the clam-faces. He empowers them, gives them weapons! Cuts off a planet invaded with their spawn from outside help. No, he is fully aware of what Bojai has become. It's inarguable."

"Yeah, well, maybe he does know," Star-Lord said. "Maybe he doesn't also want Nova attention by having the Guardians of the Galaxy disappear when their destination is known Nova business. If we didn't return from Bojai, this corner of the galaxy would be loaded with folks asking questions."

"Bah," Drax said. "Nonsense."

"Either way, Drax, what are we going to do if Z'Drut did try to have us killed, huh?" Star-Lord asked. "The odds are not fun, guys. It's looking like it's the five of us versus two . . . uh, planets. I'm just saying, I think it might be a good call to get some distance before we dive back in. Wow, I feel like a cornball even saying that."

"You're not!" Rocket cried, his voice trembling. He sniffed loudly, and then added, "I'll never question you again!"

"Dude," Star-Lord said, narrowing his eyes as he strode over to Rocket. "Are you crying?"

"I am Groot," Groot confirmed, nodding grimly.

"NO, I'M NOT!" Rocket snapped, and then let out a series of choked sobs as he directed the ship away from Bojai. "I screwed up, Quill. If I just waited like we planned, Gamora wouldn't have a chunk of face missing! We almost got killed, and it's all my fault!"

"Come on, buddy, you're fine," Star-Lord said, patting Rocket on the back as he sobbed. "You're just coming down from your post-battle high. Everyone's fine. We're all good, man. Gamora's all salved up—"

"Don't say *salved*," Gamora interjected.

"The point is," Star-Lord said, "we're good. And we'll stay good if we're all on the same page. That's all I'm saying."

Gamora walked up to the controls and knelt down next to Rocket, who was snorting wetly as he wiped his eyes.

"Rocket. Look at me," she said.

He turned to her, his eyes shining and wet.

"Am I dead?" she asked.

He narrowed his eyes. "Um. No?"

"I'm pretty sure, in my current state, I could still kick your sorry butt. Am I right?" she asked.

"Sure?"

"I'm *fine*," she said, patting him on the knee. "And Peter's right. We walked into something deeper and nastier than we could've imagined, so now, it's on us to finesse each step. At this point, with the sheer number of Thandrid back on Bojai, we can assume one of two things: that Emperor Z'Drut is fully aware of the invasion, or he and his planet are being used the same way. The way he handled our meeting suggests to me that he was fully in control of everything he was saying. And that . . . that brings us to our current problem."

"The drones," Star-Lord said.

"The drones," Gamora repeated. "They've established a force field that stretches out completely around this solar system. That leaves us with four possible directions. One, back to Bojai—obviously, not doable. Two, back to Spiralite—which, judging from this morning, isn't a much friendlier place than the chaos we just left. Three, on to Incarnadine—the only other accessible planet, though we can't be sure that they haven't already fallen to the Thandrid, too."

"That was just three," Star-Lord said. "You said four."

"I don't know if four is even possible," Gamora said.

"Well, let's hear it, because with one, two, and three, all I'm hearing is one: certain death, two: certain death or imprisonment, and three: very, very likely death," Star-Lord said.

"Four would be to attack the drones," Gamora said. "If we can turn the ship around and arc high enough to get a good shot at where the drones that impounded us came from, maybe we could shoot them down. We know that weapons and machinery can't pass through the field they're creating, but if we can damage a few of the drones creating the field, maybe we'd be able to get the *Milano* through."

"I am Groot," said Groot, gesturing toward the control board.

"Groot's right," Rocket said. "We don't have the tech to locate the drones. We'd be shooting blind like a bunch of idiots, and they'd be back on us again before we knew it."

"Agreed," Gamora said. "But if they come at us, then we don't have to keep wondering where they are, do we?"

"Yes," Drax said. "We shall draw them out."

"Because that worked so well with the Thandrid ..." Rocket said.

"If anyone has a better plan, I'm more than willing to hear it," Gamora said. After a moment of awkward silence, she clapped her hands against her legs. "Right. Let's do this."

"I'm going to take us out the far side of the system," Rocket said. "We should probably avoid a flyby of Spiralite." He turned the ship and fired the thrusters while the Guardians settled in for the trip.

"Hold up. Look at this." Gamora pointed at one of the command screens. Where they should have seen open space, they instead saw a glowing, blue expanse of what looked like water encircling them, showing a blurry and shimmering image of the stars and planets far in the distance.

"Ugh," Rocket said. "It's the damn wall. It's encircling us."

"Like some sort of interstellar snow globe, and we're just caught inside," Star-Lord said, shaking his head.

Gamora arched a brow.

"Oh," Star-Lord said. "Earth thing."

Gamora observed that, from their vantage point inside of the wall, the force field shone the same color as the flaming energy in the pit and tower back on Spiralite.

"I think the drones are powered by Spiraline energy," Gamora said. "The same stuff that they've been invaded for is what's blocking everyone out."

"Kind of poetic," Star-Lord said.

"Never been a fan of poetry, myself," Gamora said.

"I am Groot!" Groot said, pointing to the digital map at the center of the control panel.

In the three-dimensional image of the planets around them, they saw two pulsating blue dots appear on Spiralite, lifting off of the planet.

"Dammit," Rocket said, kicking the panel. "Two bogeys coming off Spiralite."

"Drones?" Gamora asked.

"Nah, these are full ships," Rocket said. "And they seem to be faster than us. I'm gonna guess they're not interested in congratulating us on our escape from their buggy buddies back on Bojai."

The ships appeared as blue sparks in the glass in front of them, getting bigger by the moment. Gamora cursed, and turned to Star-Lord. "They're coming right at us," she said. "No way we make it to the drones."

"Option three seems to be the only one where death is only *probably* the end result," Star-Lord offered with a sardonic smile.

Gamora couldn't help but chuckle. "All right. Make a dive for Incarnadine. And send some static their way as we go."

"My specialty," Rocket said, shifting around the gears and hitting a sequence of buttons on the board. The ship took a sharp right, and then Rocket gunned it. They jolted forward, speeding toward the biggest planet in the system, the ringed-giant Incarnadine.

"I'll head to the weaponry," Drax said, striding away from the deck. "We should expect hell to be waiting for us when we land. If that is the case, I'd like to give them some in return."

As they zeroed in on the gargantuan planet, with the two Thandrid crafts gaining on them, Rocket slid back a compartment on the ship that revealed a series of glowing, red buttons. He wiggled his paw. "Man the controls, Groot. Daddy's gonna make a fire."

Rocket began to stab the buttons repeatedly with his claws, cackling loudly as he tapped. Behind them, fat rings of fire shot out of the *Milano*, careening toward the Thandrid crafts. The ships, sleek and bright, wove around each flaming attack, avoiding them with apparent ease.

"You think that's all I got?" Rocket yelled.

"Gun it, man!" Star-Lord said, as Groot increased the speed. "How fast can we get there?"

"I am Groot!"

"Five minutes," Rocket said, leaning over to snatch back the controls from Groot. "Assuming there's a place to land. Should we try to establish comms with 'em?"

"No," Gamora said, holding out a hand. "Absolutely not. If they are compromised, we'd be alerting them to our arrival."

"Looks like the Thandrid already know we're onto them," Star-Lord said. "We're not exactly coming in covertly either here."

"Still," Gamora said. "Keep going, and keep shooting."

Rocket did just that. Within minutes, they'd gained a stretch of distance from the Thandrid crafts, but their enemies were still coming at them as they passed over Bojai, the rings of Incarnadine filling the field of vision from the flight deck.

They broke past Incarnadine's rings, which looked like an iridescent, rainbow halo around the planet, before entering the planet's atmosphere. With solid ground approaching quickly, Rocket slowed the ship's speed, and the Thandrid crafts were once again right behind them.

"Oh, you still want it?" Rocket barked, switching back over to the weapons panel. "You ain't seen nothing yet, you overgrown beetles!"

Just then, the ship jerked forward and to the side, as its left wing took a hit. Groot and Rocket both grasped the controls, moving to right the ship, but Gamora had taken enough fire in her life to know what had happened.

"Wing's compromised," Rocket said. "We have to get down. Now."

"We need a bit more space between us and them," Star-Lord said.

"Not gonna happen," Rocket said. "I'm gonna hit 'em with everything I got, but if we don't make ground soon, we're gonna spin out."

"Do it, then," Gamora said. "When we get out, we run for cover, and slowly head for higher ground. If we're going to beat them on foot, we need to see them from afar."

"Let's do this," Rocket said, and Groot nodded.

As Groot slowed the ship, Rocket smashed his paw on all of the buttons, and an explosion of lasers, fire, and noxious smoke blasted from the *Milano* as they descended. The Thandrid ships faltered, but shot off and away from the brunt of the blows, which disappeared into the starry sky.

Just as Rocket prepared to let out another attack, both of

the blue dots disappeared from their screen. Rocket leered at it, pressing the real-time camera. "What the . . ."

Behind them, the ships were falling out of the air, thick smoke rising off of them as they spun downward. Rocket scrunched up his face, and then let out a whooping cheer. "I did it!" he shouted.

Gamora raised a brow, watching as the ships disappeared from their cameras. "I don't think so."

"Hey," Star-Lord said, his tone suddenly bright. "If someone shot them down, maybe we have some allies here!"

"Are you kidding? That was me!" Rocket said. "Ain't you ever heard of a, uh—a delayed reaction explosion? That's absolutely a thing."

"I am Groot," Groot said, pointing ahead as the *Milano*, shaking violently, prepared to land. Now that they were closing in on solid ground, Gamora could see that the heavenly rings might have been the only beautiful thing left on the planet. It was a grey world, barren and scorched. They passed over what seemed to have once been home to an advanced civilization, but which had now been bombed and burned to rubble.

There were no people in sight.

"God, we're right in the open," Star-Lord said, pointing out a strip of ground. It was torn up, and littered with bodies. From where they were, they couldn't tell if the bodies were Thandrid or otherwise, but they'd know soon enough. "We better hope there's no one else coming our way. We're not gonna get lucky like that again."

"I don't think that was luck. This is a war zone," Gamora said. "Whoever the Incarnadinians were, they fought back."

"Not loving the past tense there, gotta say," Star-Lord said.

Gamora shared a grim look with him. "Me neither."

They landed in a series of four harsh, scrapping bounces. Star-Lord cringed, and Gamora knew he was imagining the damage done to the ship—and she couldn't help but feel the same. She'd never taken pride in a spacecraft before knowing Peter Quill, but he'd made the *Milano* more than just transport. It was home.

But for now, it was grounded. And, until they figured something out, so were they.

After scanning the area on their maps and finding that the last record of this city was a far cry from the war-torn stretch of devastation in which they'd landed, they headed to the port. They'd agreed that reaching out to contact the Incarnadinians was too risky, even though the destruction of the Thandrid crafts gave them hope that they had allies laying in wait within the city's confines. Drax gave each of them as many weapons as they could strap to themselves. Preparing for the worst, but not wanting to prolong the tension of not knowing exactly what waited for them on this planet, Gamora went to open the port, but then hesitated.

She looked back at her friends. "As soon as we hit the

ground, we get as far away from the ship as we can. Once we're a fair distance, we search for possible shelter or any functioning facilities. Our best bet would be, if we can find a functioning comm device with more power than our ship has, to contact the Nova Corps and alert them to what's going on here. We do not engage if we don't have to. We do not stay. If we don't find anything worthwhile in five minutes, we head out of the city and for the hills. Agreed?"

"Agreed," Star-Lord said. "Also, just throwing it out there . . . if someone on this planet really did shoot those crafts down, we might want to find them. Assuming that the war they've been fighting is against the Thandrid, we're gonna want them on our side if we want to somehow take down that drone wall."

"Let's go," Gamora said, and pulled open the port.

They stepped out and onto the burnt ground. There were Thandrid corpses littering the area, but also the bodies of humanoid aliens with skin that must have once resembled the lustrous color of the planet's rings: Incarnadinians. Now, though, they were mostly painted with a layer of dirt, and a thick blue substance that Gamora was certain was their blood.

The Guardians of the Galaxy advanced, weapons drawn, but it seemed that there was no one left here to fight. Together, they stepped away from the ship and began to make their way toward the ruined city, its buildings stretching up to the sky like broken, hollow bones. It seemed that they were alone in the area—until it became all too clear that they weren't.

A bright floodlight suddenly illuminated the area, blinding the five of them. The Guardians pointed their guns and blades up, trying to squint through the glaring light to see their attackers, but it was so bright that it burned just to open their eyes.

Gamora prepared to call out to whoever was targeting them, but a booming, powerful, female voice sounded, seeming to fill the entire field.

"Drop your weapons and surrender to the Rebel Queen," the voice boomed. "Or you will be immediately executed."

CHAPTER NINE

Understanding

Groot

Groot hoped that Gamora was right to lay down her weapons.

He currently sat alone on a stool in what he believed an underground bunker. Through the thick, stone walls, Groot heard muffled voices coming from a fair distance, but he couldn't be sure if they belonged to his friends or their captors. He had been waiting patiently, growing and shrinking a flower on his palm over and over again in the empty, dank room for what felt like hours—just long enough to allow his imagination to run wild. He fought the impulse to charge out of the room to check on his friends, reminding himself over and over that Gamora was wise. Truly, if anyone could navigate them out of the war in which they'd found themselves embroiled, it was her, the fallen daughter of Thanos and the last remaining Zen-Whoberian.

When the so-called Rebel Queen's voice commanded them to drop their weapons, Gamora had indeed been the first to kneel to the ground. Both Star-Lord and Rocket had balked, but Drax, normally ready to fight, had met Gamora's eye and then proceeded to shed his own weaponry. An army of Incarnadinians, their pearly skin shimmering a different color with every step, as luminescent and beautiful as the rings that made this war-torn planet seem something other than dead, came out of the surrounding buildings with rifles trained on the Guardians. They were humanoid, not very tall like the Bojaians nor small like the Spiralines—and certainly nothing like the Thandrid. Groot raised his hands in surrender, trusting in Gamora's plan, whatever it was. After Star-Lord and Rocket finally acquiesced, the Incarnadinians blindfolded the five of them and led them across the ruined cityscape and down into the musty bunker in which Groot now sat. When they removed the rag they'd tied around Groot's face and walked out without another word, Groot was alone. He suspected the same had happened to his friends.

Presently, he looked up as the heavy stone door scraped open, and a female Incarnadinian entered. She wore a sleek, emerald-green uniform with an armored chestplate, a leathery collar that reached all the way to her cheekbones, framing her heart-shaped face, and a belt lined with a series of short blades, most of them thin and small, more like the tools of a surgeon than the weapons of a warrior. What was not thin, however, was the gun, long as a sword, strapped to her left side.

All of the Incarnadinians that Groot had seen so far had the same iridescent skin and pale hair of varying colors—

periwinkle, lavender, sea-foam green—but this woman was the only one on whom Groot had seen pure white hair. It came down in ropey stands over her wide, crystalline-white eyes, which bore into Groot.

"Hello, there," she said, and Groot instantly recognized her voice. She was the one who had commanded them to drop their weapons.

The so-called Rebel Queen.

"I am Groot."

The Rebel Queen stared at Groot, who began to feel a creeping sense of trepidation. He understood all at once what this was: an interrogation. Considering how limited his communication skills were, those never quite went well for him. He began thinking about how he could successfully use charades to mime "I need Rocket to translate for me" when the Rebel Queen broke her silence.

"And how are you doing today?"

Groot sighed. This was where he knew it would go bad. He looked her straight on and said, "I am Groot." Which meant *If I'm being honest, today has been a nightmare.*

To Groot's surprise, the Rebel Queen nodded with understanding. "I understand, and share your sentiment. Pain is momentary . . . until it is not."

Groot stared at her, dumbfounded.

She reached out a four-fingered hand. "My name is Jesair."

Groot took her hand in his own, his roots snaking around

hers as she gave him a firm shake. "I am Groot?" he asked. *You understand me?*

"Indeed," she said, a prim smile spreading across her lips. "I must apologize. Do you not have a translator implant?"

"I am . . . Groot . . ." *I do. It's merely that many others . . . almost everyone, in fact . . . cannot decipher my words, even translated. Only Rocket.*

She closed her eyes, nodding with understanding. "I forget how wide and varied the universe continues to be. Of course, of course. Not every being communicates on . . . how can I say this, in a way that would exist in a line . . ."

"I am Groot?" *Exist in a line?*

"It's an expression," Jesair said. "Referring to the way non-Incarnadinians communicate. I hope you don't take offense."

Groot shook his head.

"See, Incarnadinians are melolinguists," she said. "To 'exist in a line' is to listen to speech and decipher a meaning. Incarnadinians *take in* speech. We read the face, the tone, the words, the thought, the soul. It sounds, perhaps, poetic . . . but I assure you, I'm not being whimsical. It is a science to us, and one that we have come to embrace as a people."

"I . . . am Groot." *I'm so pleased to speak with someone who can understand me. It . . . has been a long time since my thoughts have been clear to anyone but myself and my closest friend.*

"It's important to be heard, and more important yet, to be understood," Jesair said. "So much of who we are is what we say."

"I am Groot." *How true. I sometimes wonder if, because of the way I limit my speech due to the fact that no one can under-stand me, if I have somehow become less "me."*

"I understand, Groot. Would you be comfortable, then, if I asked you a few questions?"

Groot inclined his head.

"Your ship—which is currently safely in storage, and on its way toward being repaired by my best engineers—was spot-ted by my mappers leaving the planet Bojai. You and your crew then journeyed toward the planet Spiralite, before turn-ing back toward Incarnadine, accompanied by two Thandrid crafts. What was your business on Bojai, and what made you about-face and approach my planet?"

"I am Groot," Groot explained. *We had been tasked with delivering medical supplies to Bojai, but were ambushed by a horde of Thandrid while there. Knowing that we were trapped in this solar system by Spiralite's drones, we attempted to pin-point and fire at the drones, but were apprehended by the Than-drid ships.* Groot sighed, and added, "I am Groot." *We thought that Incarnadine, the only planet we weren't certain was occu-pied by the Thandrid, was our only safe bet, though I can now see that we brought trouble to your home. My deepest apologies.*

"You see that we have suffered here on Incarnadine," Jesair said. It wasn't a question.

"I am Groot." *I don't merely see it. I can feel it.*

Jesair inclined her head. Groot was unsure if she was moved

by his comment or if she was thinking of the next question she'd ask, but his fear that his friends were being tortured in the other rooms had been alleviated.

"I believe you," Jesair said. "I've spoken to all members of your crew and, while the small one was perhaps the most lined speaker I've ever encountered, I empathize with your situation. You have walked into a hall with three doors, each with a different horror waiting within. After your experiences, it would've been understandable for you to act toward my command with hostility, but instead, you humbly lowered your weapons. You have shown that you mean this world no harm."

"I am Groot." *I mean no world harm.*

"Harm is not an inherently evil concept," Jesair said. "It can be well earned. Do you disagree?"

"I am Groot . . ." *I agree that sometimes harm must be done, yes. It is never my intention to deal pain, though. If there is another way, that is . . .*

"But you are a warrior," Jesair said with a smile. "I can see it etched on your skin, deep in your eyes. The absence of malice does not equate to the presence of weakness. You, Groot, have done and seen much. Do you know what lies ahead?"

Groot looked at Jesair, trying to decide what to say. It had been a long time since he'd had to choose his words so carefully. As freeing as it was, it was also a challenge for him to find the exact word to shape around his meaning. It cut deeper, even, than what he'd said to Jesair. He felt almost as if being understood as someone who only said three words had become his default, a mask that he had worn for so long that he became comfortable hiding behind it. Now, now that he was being understood, seen without that mask, he had to ask himself: *Who* am *I, after all?*

"I am Groot," he said. *I cannot say what lies ahead. I hope for peace, but hope dwindles. I fear that evil will force our hand.*

"'Our,'" Jesair repeated. "Who do you mean?"

"I am Groot." *The Guardians of the Galaxy.*

"Star-Lord mentioned that . . . he was surprised that I hadn't heard of you," Jesair said. "No offense."

Groot chuckled.

"You are right to fear what you fear, though, Groot," Jesair said. "I don't mean to be fatalistic. War consumes much, but it does not consume all. My home is ravaged, but the damage does not come from the Thandrid alone. My people—my rebels—we fought our invaders at every step. It has cost us much of this planet, but every day, we drive more of them back."

"I am Groot?" *Do you know their plan?*

"Yes," Jesair said. "But before we discuss what we've learned, I have one final question for you, Groot."

"I am Groot." *I'm happy to answer.*

"Would you die to keep the ones you love safe?"

Groot held her gaze for a prolonged moment. Quietly, he said, "I am Groot."

She breathed in satisfied. "Well, Groot . . . so would I. I believe we hold that interest in common, and that we both know what we have to do to make sure those we care for deepest, those whose souls *live* at the core of our being, continue in this life."

"I am Groot." *I do know. We'll fight.*

"Yes," Jesair said. "But first . . . we'll drink."

CHAPTER TEN

Big Giant Crybaby

Drax

"Tomorrow, we wage war . . ." Drax said, his voice a grave, menacing growl. He looked across the dimly lit, makeshift pub from Groot, to Rocket, to Gamora, to Star-Lord, to the many Incarnadinian rebels, and then, finally, to Jesair, whose stare he held before he beat his fist on his chest with ferocity. Then, with his other hand, he lifted his mug into the air, green liquid sloshing over the rim and raining down on the bar. "TONIGHT, WE ENGAGE IN MERRIMENT!"

Everyone in the room echoed his gesture with a thunderous cheer, and then drank the contents of their mugs. Drax slammed his down on the bar—a table stacked on another table—and slid it over to the bartender, who had moments earlier introduced himself as one of Jesair's generals.

The truth was, it wasn't so much a bar as it was one of the only buildings in the city that was still structurally sound enough in which to gather. The walls were made of a material much like concrete, sturdy and thick, but even so, there were burn marks on the wall in areas. Drax pictured a firefight between the Thandrid and Incarnadinians within these very walls, and his hatred for the insectoid species swelled.

Jesair strode over to Drax as the room filled with chatter. "A lovely toast," she said. "Incarnadinians tend to use toasts as a platform with which to expound on topics such as the nature of life, its continuity with death, and so on. We may have waited until sunrise to break if not for you. Thank you for your brevity."

Drax grunted, and then smiled.

"Your sustenance," the bartender said, placing the mug, newly filled, in front of Drax.

"An odd name for ale," Drax said, nodding his gratitude to the bartending general.

"Oh, it's not ale," Jesair said. "Well, it's not *merely* ale. It's everything."

Drax removed his lips from the drink. He wasn't entirely sure of Jesair's meaning, but he *did* know that, while he had ingested a copious amount of foul things to nourish himself over the years when food was scarce, he wouldn't dare eat *anything*—and most certainly not everything. "Your meaning?"

Jesair sipped her own beverage. "Our food is our drink is our medication is our life," she said. She inclined her cup. "We have only this. We need only this."

"So . . ." Drax said. "If this 'sustenance' is also medication, if I drink too much, drinking *more* would cure me of any sickness."

"An odd way of looking at it, but yes," Jesair said. "Do you like it?"

Drax nodded heartily. It tasted clean and tickled his throat with its bubbles. Unlike the buzz of alcohol, this drink made everything brighter, sharper. He noticed, then, in the heightened clarity that the drink offered, that Jesair was quite beautiful. He'd originally thought her eyes to be pure white, but he saw now that they, like her skin, reflected the prism of light around her, catching all of it and sending its beauty back at everyone who looked at her. Drax wondered what it would feel like to touch the skin of her cheek.

"What?" she asked, narrowing her eyes. "Have I something on my face?"

"Nothing!" Drax stood up and turned away, his eyes wide as he scanned the room. He located Star-Lord leaning on a table, talking animatedly to two Incarnadinian women. "Excuse me. I think that I heard someone call me. 'Drax,' they said. 'Come here . . . now.'"

"Oh," Jesair said, baffled. "I—"

Drax turned away before she could finish her sentence and made a beeline for Star-Lord. He weaved in between a group of Incarnadinians, some of who appeared to be frightened of him, while others offered him genuine smiles. As soon as Drax was in earshot of Star-Lord, he shouted: "PETER QUILL!"

"Oh, hey, Drax. You're sounding . . . fully sustained," Star-Lord said, taking a sip of his drink. "What's up, bud?"

"Repeat the story you were just sharing with these ladies you're attempting to impress," he said, forcing a smile as he clapped Star-Lord on the back, sending him sprawling forward. The entire contents of his mug splashed out onto the two Incarnadinian women, who leapt from their seats as the drink drenched them.

They stood, shot Drax a pair of dirty looks, and turned without another word, striding toward the bartender, who had seen the spill and was already grabbing a grungy towel.

Star-Lord stared after them, silently mouthing words of protest. With a great sigh, Drax sat where they'd been and put his mug down on the table. He patted the seat next to him.

"Dude, what are you doing?" Star-Lord said.

"This gesture," Drax said, patting the bench again with cartoonishly exaggerated movements, "represents a request for you to sit."

"I know what it—you know what, never mind," Star-Lord said, leaning toward Drax. "I was right in the middle of telling them the story about the Thandrid on Bojai. I was getting to the part where I did that trick shot and blasted three at once, before you doused them."

"I didn't douse them," Drax said. "You are the douser."

"Let's do the math. Two minutes ago, I had a full drink, and was hanging out with the two hottest rebels in the room— maybe on the planet! Now, I'm drinkless and I'm talking to you. *You* are for sure the douser."

Drax stood, sending the bench flying back as he stepped toward Star-Lord with pure menace in his gaze. "They . . . were *not* the most beautiful rebels in the room!"

Star-Lord scrunched his face, taking a step back from Drax. A few of the Incarnadinians close to them watched, baffled.

"Drax," Star-Lord said. "What's up? What happened? I don't wanna say you're acting crazy, buuuuuut you're not acting *not* crazy."

Drax's cold eyes bore into Star-Lord's for a moment, before he deflated, shaking his head. "I have now made a fool of myself twice this evening."

Star-Lord grabbed the bench and stood it back upright. He sat down and then, looking up at Drax, patted the seat.

Drax sat.

"I'm sure you—uh, we—could apologize to those two," Star-Lord said. "They seemed super cool, so I don't think you have anything to worry about. They're way more concerned with, you know, dying in a hail of Spiraline lasers than getting doused. Promise."

"I'm not referring to them!" Drax said, slamming his fist against the table. He looked over to Star-Lord and then, as subtly as he could, jerked his head toward the other side of the pub.

He and Star-Lord looked up to see Jesair laughing with Groot and Rocket.

"What, the Rebel Queen?" Star-Lord said. "What did you say to her that was so bad?"

Drax spoke through gritted teeth. "If you tell another living being, you will no longer be such yourself."

"What's your deal, man?" Star-Lord asked. "What can you tell me that I don't already know about you? Remember that time we fought the bog-dragon and its acid breath incinerated your clothes? I have *that* image burned into my memory forever. I promise, nothing you could say will top that."

Drax clenched his jaw, tilting his head back. "I am ashamed."

"Come on," Star-Lord said, his voice softening. "Jokes aside, we almost died today. Together. Because that's how we do things, right?"

Drax looked him in the eye, and this time, he chuckled. "Yes. You are right." He lowered his voice and leaned in to Star-Lord. "It began when Jesair was interrogating me. I knew the value in Gamora's choice, that our only hope out of this situation was to find an ally in the Incarnadinians. I answered all of her questions, and I swore fealty until we could, together, escape this problem."

"Yeah, me too," Star-Lord said. "We all did. I think Rocket may have insulted her a few times first, is what I heard, but they seem okay now."

"That is not it," Drax said. "When Jesair revealed the full scope of the Thandrid plan, it got . . ."

"It got what?"

Drax's voice dropped even lower, to a barely audible whisper. "Personal."

* * *

Two hours earlier, Drax sat across from Jesair, answering her questions and listening to her strong, melodic voice.

"You understand, then, the extent of the horror that has gripped our solar system?" Jesair asked Drax, who had thus far used as few words as possible to answer her questions. She spoke in flowery language, much of which Drax didn't understand, and he fought the urge to search for meaning in her turns of phrase. He may not have been able to understand all figures of speech, but he had gotten rather good at noticing *when* someone might be using one.

Jesair, however, was very hard for him to figure out.

"I understand," Drax said. He thought for a moment, and then added, "I understand that the Thandrid have a different use for each planet. I understand that you are fighting back. I understand *that* best of all."

"Yes, Drax," Jesair said. "For someone who names himself 'Destroyer,' you are quite the illuminated thinker. Allow me to illuminate the situation further . . ."

"Shine your light," Drax said.

"The Thandrid are a warrior race, as you have likely noticed from your battle with them on Bojai," Jesair said. "They are based out of Spiralite, and have formed an alliance with that planet's emperor . . . Z'Drut. Though we still don't know the extent of their alliance, whether it be one of choice or a forced takeover, early spy missions have confirmed that the drone wall cloaking our solar system from the rest of the universe is powered by Spiraline energy."

"How long has this been going on?" Drax asked.

"To our knowledge, it began around two months ago," Jesair said.

Two months. That was around the same time, Drax thought to himself, that Kairmi Har had told Star-Lord was when the Bojaians had begun showing symptoms of a neurological plague. Drax said, "So Bojai was attacked first, then."

"In retrospect, it seems that is the case. We didn't know, then, about the truth of Bojai's troubles. We still don't know how long this plan has been in place. You see, Spiralite has been in a bad position for quite some time. Their energy source was so valuable it attracted many aggressive species attempting to use it to their own ends, which led to many devastating invasions stretching back longer than our written word. My husband, the king . . . when he was alive . . . offered Spiralite his help. We were allies—uneasy, yes, as Z'Drut never trusted Incarnadine, but allies nonetheless. Instead of accepting our offer, they sought their alliance with the Thandrid . . . but perhaps this has been in the works for far longer than any of us know."

Drax looked up at her. "How was your husband killed?"

Jesair was silent for a moment. Drax watched her, wondering how different her thoughts must be than his own. There seemed to be an unfathomable gulf between them, Jesair with her incomprehensible words and ideas, and him, Drax. But then, when she spoke to Drax again, she suddenly seemed far from unfathomable.

"On Incarnadine, there is no distinction between a king and a general and a warrior. I say this not to extol the virtues of my people's elected leaders, but to explain why he was where he was," Jesair said. "His name was Irn, and he was beautiful in mind, deep in soul. When trouble first began to make itself known on Bojai, in what both Bojai and we believed was a sickness rather than an invasion, Irn was among the first of the aforementioned 'spies' to journey to the planet in hopes of discovering the source of our neighbor's troubles. When he saw the Thandrid, and began to wonder if they were connected to the sickness, he attempted to alert the Bojaian hierarchy, but he was attacked. His men, slaughtered. He made it to his ship with one other, and our footage, fed to a now-destroyed command central from their ship, shows them landing near the emperor's facility on Spiralite. They never returned."

Drax looked at her pearlescent eyes, gleaming with the light of the room, as she paused, breathed in deeply, and then continued.

"Shortly after that, the attacks began on Incarnadine," Jesair said. "Armed with Spiraline energy, the Thandrid attacked our cities, unleashing a series of ground attacks that would culminate in a massive invasion a month later . . . and that is when the drone wall went up. Now, cut off from the larger universe, the Thandrid attack us freely and in full force. I have traveled wide, gathering rebel forces from my cities' survivors to fight back through the decimation . . . but the Thandrid numbers seem to grow daily."

Drax narrowed his eyes. "Your husband . . ."

"Yes?"

"You never saw him die," Drax said. "Z'Drut keeps a prison, and it is full of many different—"

"I didn't see him die, but I saw footage of Emperor Z'Drut, along with his Thandrid guard, executing my people." She paused a moment before going on. "The Spiralines operate within a caste system, with the emperor as the highest good. He would see my Irn as the same, and a greater enemy than the warriors he saw fit to kill. My husband . . ." Jesair said, fresh pain in her voice, "is dead."

Before he could stop himself, Drax extended his hand. "My wife . . ." he said, a slight tremble in his voice. "My children."

Jesair took his hand. Her touch was soft, warm to the touch. Strong. As he held her hand for that moment, Drax felt his eyes sting with tears.

He pulled his hand back and stood abruptly, turning away from Jesair. He coughed. "S-sorry. I—I am getting over a cold."

"I wish you well," she said softly.

Drax, his back still facing her, said, after a long pause, "And I wish you the same . . ."

"Wait, so you cried?" Star-Lord said.

Drax grabbed him by the shirt and pulled him close. His upper lip curling with rage, he said, "You dare mock me after I shared my tale?"

"Not mocking! Totally not mocking!" Star-Lord said. "Listen, man—crying? Not a big deal! You've seen me cry before. Right? I cry. We all cry, dude."

Drax narrowed his eyes. "This is true?"

"This is true," Star-Lord said, pulling himself free from Drax's grasp. "I teared up a little bit earlier on when Groot gave Gamora a big ol' hug. It's normal to cry. It doesn't make you *not* Drax the Destroyer. It just makes you also Drax the . . ." Star-Lord took a big step back. ". . . big giant crybaby."

Drax reached for Star-Lord, roaring, but Star-Lord held out his hands, laughing. "I'm kidding! I promise, next time I cry, I'll let you know. It'll be a moment. We'll share it."

With a great sigh, Drax nodded. ". . . Yes. That sounds excellent."

"Hey, wait a second," Star-Lord said, sliding back over to him. "You said you made a fool of yourself *twice*. What was the other time?"

Drax nudged his head, once again, toward Jesair.

"*Again?*" Star-Lord said. "What did you do?"

"I abruptly ended a lovely conversation," Drax said.

"... Did you just say 'lovely conversation'?" Star-Lord asked.

"The Rebel Queen ... Jesair ... speaking with her makes my head and my chest feel a ... a rush of thoughts," Drax said, grasping for words. "She ... she makes me think, and speak, and feel outside of who I am. Outside of Drax the Destroyer."

"Whoa," Star-Lord said. "If I had just an inch left of self-control, I'd be calling Gamora over to hear you right now. You're not Drax the Big Giant Crybaby, man. You're Drax the Lover."

"You speak nonsense," Drax snapped.

"*You* speak nonsense!" Star-Lord said, grinning. "If you heard yourself, you'd be all 'How can a brain feel a rush? How can one be outside of themselves?' You're in love with the Rebel Queen, man."

"No," Drax said. He looked at Star-Lord, shaking his head. "I will never feel love again. This is not that."

"Then what is it?" Star-Lord asked.

Drax peered across the bar once again and watched as Jesair spoke animatedly with Groot and Rocket, her smiling shining, her eyes cheerful, her skin catching the dim light of the room and reflecting it back twice as bright.

"A kindred soul," Drax said.

* * *

Later that night, as the merriment died down and the rebels began to prepare for the night watch, Jesair gathered the Guardians of the Galaxy and led them to a bunker that was far nicer than the makeshift bar, which Drax suspected had been a courthouse before the city had been devastated by war. The bunker across the way was warmer than any building they'd been in before, and even had enough electricity to line the walls with a dim but consistent glow. It flickered, but it was something.

"We have a hidden guard watching the area, as you experienced when you landed," Jesair said. "We see everything that passes through these skies, and this city is seeded with warriors waiting for the slightest hint of an enemy. You may rest here in peace, without fear of attack."

"Rest in peace," Rocket said. "Yikes. Not the best choice of words, lady."

Drax glared at him.

"Ah. A colloquialism which I'm unaware of, though I see the meaning plain on your face," Jesair said to Rocket with a laugh. "You will certainly not die on my watch."

"Queen Jesair, if I may . . ." Gamora said. "We've established that my team will help your people, and vice versa, in this battle—but we haven't quite gone over a plan."

"Ah. Time is of the essence for you," Jesair said. "I understand, Gamora. Where our battle is an existential one, yours is fleeting. You will move on from this world, and would like to do so with haste."

"I don't mean offense," Gamora said.

"And I take none," Jesair said. "We are so much more than our words . . . but I will give you mine, in hopes that they ease your mind enough to dream deeply tonight. In order to stop the Thandrid before they become an indomitable empire in the model of the Skrulls, the Kree, and the Chitauri, as it seems they plan to do, we must expose their actions to the universe at large. Their ranks have already grown too vast for any other recourse."

"I am Groot," Groot said.

"Exactly. The wall of drones," Jesair said. "They keep us from communicating just as they keep people from seeing in. Once the drones come down, the evils of the Thandrid will be exposed. A universe of allies exists, unaware of our troubles."

"Do you have weapons powerful enough to locate and shoot the drones?" Star-Lord asked. "That's what we were trying to do."

"I'm afraid not," Jesair said. "They are hidden from sight, and spread throughout the solar system. They would need to be disabled from a central location, though I know not if any one place exists. Perhaps within Z'Drut's offices, though I cannot claim to know."

"The tower . . ." Drax said, narrowing his eyes. He looked

up, startled to see all of their eyes locked on him. "Jesair had spoken earlier of an idea that the drones were powered by the natural energy from Spiralite. It burned most brightly in the tower."

"Also, whatever they were mining around the prison . . . " Rocket added.

"Not like at the tower," Drax said. "I believe that the work being done at the prison mine is a means by which to tap into the planet's energy in order to foster it . . . much like drilling for oil. But that tower . . . that is a channel for the power, once it's gathered. Its glow is brighter on Spiralite than even the light of the sun."

"Well, if that really is the spot, maybe we could bomb the tower," Star-Lord suggested. "Rocket, you must have a good supply still, right?"

"Nothin' that would shoot from here. We'd need to get real close anyway, 'cause those drones are mobile. If they could impound our ship like that, you bet they could track a bomb coming at 'em. Nah, we'd need to be right near the target," Rocket said. "And it seems once we get close enough to do damage, they're already on us."

Drax turned to Groot. "You saw a ship on Spiralite carting off dead Thandrid."

"I am Groot."

"He said 'Either dead, or perhaps just injured,'" Jesair said. "And yes, I can attest to this. When the Thandrid attack, they often have another ship that collects their dead. They don't often come to our stronghold here to do so, but when Thandrid are killed on the outskirts or other battlefields, yes."

"What for?" Rocket asked.

"They are a deeply religious species, from what I understand," Jesair said. "I cannot know for sure, but I have seen evidence in the battlefields that they eat their dead in a cannibalistic ritual that—"

"Whoa," Rocket said. "You know, I'm all good on my Thandrid knowledge. From the face-sacs to the head babies to their eat-a-friend diet, I don't think I need any more info, thanks."

Jesair sighed. "They are complex beings, as convenient as it would be to rob them of that."

"You believe that they will be along to collect the bodies within those ships your people shot down?" Drax asked. "The ships that were following us."

"Most assuredly," Jesair said. "They make regular runs to pick up the bodies, though they struggle to keep up. Our warriors keep them busy. But they will certainly retrieve the dead from the ships first, as they fell outside the city."

Drax grinned. "Then our course of action is set."

"Wait, what?" Rocket said. "Am I missing something?"

"Drax, you're a genius," Gamora said, beaming. "Absolutely brilliant."

"What is everyone talking about? Hit me with the exposition, would ya?!" Rocket barked.

"If we can ambush the Thandrid without harming the ship, we can use it to return to Spiralite, passing through without detection," Drax said. "If we can position the ship so that we get a good shot at the energy tower . . . we can destroy it."

"Stellar," Jesair said. "A plan worthy of a warrior such as yourself. Thank you, Drax."

"Wait, wait, wait," Star-Lord said. "We're assuming there's not, like, some kind of facial scan, or alien-proof touch pad, or *something* in that ship. These things are telepathic anyway, so maybe they fly it with their minds! We don't know that this is going to work."

"Perhaps not," Jesair said. "But come morning, we will try."

"And if we fail?" Gamora asked.

"I have failed many times," Jesair said. "And yet, I stand." She turned to Drax. "Thank you once again, Drax. It is a sound plan."

Drax smiled at her, and she reached out to grab his hand again. As he took it, this time, he didn't turn away.

CHAPTER ELEVEN

On the Other Side

Gamora

The next day, Gamora was the first among her friends to rise from slumber. To her surprise, the pain she'd fallen asleep fighting had greatly waned. She touched the bridge of her nose and, feeling no more than a thin, raised lip of a cut, moved her hand down to her bicep, which was smooth but for a slick patch where, hours ago, an open cut had been.

"Hell of a drink," Gamora murmured to herself, thinking back to the many cups of Incarnadinian "sustenance" she'd enjoyed the night before. Being the warrior she was, her next thought was that such a potent medicinal tool would be invaluable during a war. Though, from what she'd seen of Incarnadine, its conflicts with the Thandrid weren't leaving many soldiers merely injured.

Gamora was pleased to count the Rebel Queen and her ranks as allies. Dire as their situation remained, together they had a fighting chance—and that was something. The last thing she'd expected after the charade Emperor Z'Drut had acted out on Spiralite and then the brutal assault on the fallen planet of Bojai was to be greeted on Incarnadine with drinks, laughter, and friendship. That was the thing about combat, though. She'd been through it many times, and heard more than her share of self-proclaimed war-time poets attempting to chronicle their planet's epic tales, recalling stories of violence and of people stripped of what made them civil, made to fight like animals for their lives. There were wars like that, of course, but that wasn't what Gamora had experienced. Not on Incarnadine, not in her time as a Guardian of the Galaxy, and not in the life she had lived before.

When people were at war, they lived for those fleeting moments of laughter, light, and life. Perhaps she shouldn't have been surprised at all to be so quickly embraced by Jesair and her people. Gamora and her friends had come there, after all, as a last possible recourse, hoping that there was something good left in their corner of the galaxy. It just so happened to turn out that there were others out there hoping for the same thing.

As Gamora watched her friends begin to wake, she made a silent promise to herself not to let them down. Not her crew, nor the Incarnadinians. She'd seen evil win far too many times, and it was so easy to forget how much good there was in the universe, waiting, reaching for something to help them fight back.

Today, Gamora promised silently, *the rebels win.*

* * *

After a quick breakfast of the same thick, green liquid, a team of Incarnadinian rebels brought the Guardians of the Galaxy back to the bunker where they'd been questioned by Jesair. There, they were shown to the storage locker where their weapons had been stored. They strapped themselves up with the swords, guns, lasers, and rocket launchers and then met back up with Jesair and a team of eight Incarnadinian rebels outside. Dust swirled in the air, but from the way that the planet's incandescent rings cast an array of vibrant colors across the ruined cityscape, Gamora couldn't help but marvel at how beautiful the planet remained even through the devastation.

"Good morning to you all," Jesair said, her voice clear and powerful. "I hope you slept well, and I thank you for joining me on this day. I have news to share . . . three Thandrid crafts have been observed by my watchers leaving Spiralite and landing on Bojai this morning."

Gamora had a sudden image of Emperor Z'Drut in her mind as she spoke—he was every bit Jesair's opposite, each of his words chosen in attempt to mask his true intent. When Jesair spoke, Gamora knew that there was no gap between what she felt and what she said. In the past, Gamora might have considered that a weakness. Z'Drut, after all, seemed to have the upper hand between the two of them, whatever his end goal be. Gamora knew, though, that there was honor in trusting others, and that leaders and warriors both were stronger when they felt loss deeply.

Jesair continued: "Some time ago, those Thandrid began to journey toward Incarnadine. They will enter our skies within moments."

"The Thandrid must know you're watching," Drax said. "Do they not care to uphold the element of surprise?"

"They used to," Jesair said. "It troubles me that they no longer do. While our stronghold over this city remains, the enemy knows that this war has not gone in our favor. To them, we've lost."

"You haven't," Drax said. "*We* haven't. Not yet. Not ever."

"How many of them fit in one craft?" Gamora asked.

"Sometimes as few as three have ridden in one vessel, sometimes as many as fifteen," Jesair said. "Only one of the ships will come for their dead, though. The others, based on observed behavior, will attack. Our group will move toward the debris of yesterday's fallen ships—a walk of no more than three minutes for us. We can expect the pickup ship to land there. Meanwhile, I have a second team—larger—set up west of us, to the distance. When the Thandrid crafts are within range, they will engage in a firefight, drawing the warships away from the pickup. When the pickup lands and the other two ships are at a safe distance, we will attack."

"And then, we ride that sucker back to Spiralite!" Rocket interjected, pointing excitedly to the clunky cannon strapped to his back. It was twice his size, jutting out from his sides like hideous wings, and had a barrel big enough for Groot to stick his whole head into. "This baby right here is what I like to call the Y.G.A.F.P.S.Y.W.P.O.F. 6000."

"The . . . *what*?" Gamora asked.

"Y.G.A.F.P.S.Y.W.P.O.F. 6000," Rocket repeated. "For dummies, that's the 'You Got A Freakin' Problem, Scumbag, Your Whole Planet's On Fire!'"

Drax furrowed his brow. "Why 6000?"

Rocket shrugged. "Sounded cool."

"I told him just to call it the Ooga-chaka, but nope," Star-Lord said. "He had to go with the A.B.C.D.E.F.G. 600."

"This initialism has the power to destroy the Spiraline energy tower?" Jesair asked.

"Smokin' crater," Rocket said, giving its wide barrel a tender stroke. "Only catch is, we've got to be close, or the fireball it blasts out will go kablooey before it hits the target."

"Which, also a better name," Star-Lord added.

"If it takes down those drones, I don't care if he calls it 'sweetheart,'" Gamora said. Then, she turned to the Rebel Queen. "Queen Jesair, if there are any surprises and this doesn't go the way we're hoping . . . we should have a chain of command. We're guests on your planet, and I'm more than happy to fall in line."

"Me too," Star-Lord said.

"It would be my honor," Drax said, his tone uncharacteristically reverential.

"I am Groot," Groot said.

"S'long as I get to pop that tower and watch it fall on Z'Drut's stupid face, I'll do whatever anyone says," Rocket said.

"You are humble and brave," Jesair said. "On Incarnadine, we act as one. Equal. All ideas are as powerful as the next. It is I, though, who will follow your lead once we make the final journey to Spiralite. With your recent experience there, I do believe that you five would know the way around better than me or my people."

"Good with me," Star-Lord said. "Though, I think we can all agree that as soon as the drone wall comes down, we haul ass out of there and get some outside help."

"Absolutely," Gamora said.

A loud crack rang through the air, and Jesair turned her eyes skyward. "The signal," she said. "The Thandrid crafts approach."

Jesair led the way, walking next to Drax, as they crept along a series of ruined buildings, making their journey toward the site at which the Thandrid crafts had been shot down the day before. Gamora couldn't hear what they were saying, but she noticed a surprising amount of smiles and softly spoken words shared between her comrade and the Rebel Queen. Normally, Drax regarded aliens they met on their journeys with either utter contempt, inappropriate amusement, or complete befuddlement. What she was seeing with him and Jesair was new, and she had to admit, she liked to see her friend smile.

She turned to Star-Lord and tapped his arm. "Look at that. Is it just me, or is Drax . . . I don't want to say flirting, but I haven't seen him smile like that in . . . well, maybe ever."

Star-Lord stared ahead, wide eyed, his jaw clenched.

"Quill, did you hear me?" Gamora asked.

Star-Lord bit his lips. "About to hijack a ship. Gotta stay focused. Can't talk about what I don't know."

Gamora gaped at him. "What are you not telling me?"

"Drax cried!" Star-Lord blurted, and then brought his hands to his mouth. He winced, shaking his head, and then turned to Gamora, talking in a low and hurried voice. "Dammit. I wasn't supposed to say anything. Drax cried and he's totally into her and I am a complete clod of dirt for saying it. A clod of dirty dirt. But why would he trust *me* with a secret? What about me inspired him to tell me this? I tell you everything, Gamora. Hell, I tell Rocket everything, and he's a bipedal raccoon who is debatably in romantic love with his guns, sooooo. . ."

Gamora lifted a single brow. "You know what? I am thoroughly sorry that I asked. Carry on."

"I'm just a little jumbly about this," Star-Lord said. "I kinda thought there'd be more . . . you know, putting our heads together, planning. All of this just seems less military and more . . . more . . ."

"Something that you would do?" Gamora asked.

"Exactly that. Except, like . . . large scale."

"Well, you're alive, aren't you?"

"Yeah, but I'm also just a dude," Star-Lord said. "Just an incredibly dashing, quick-on-his-feet, hard-to-kill, dream-date of a dude, yeah, but still—dude. This is high stakes. I'm seeing a single way that we win this, and a whole big slew of ways we don't."

"I'm with you," Gamora said. "I am. I feel the same way. I wish we had more time to think this through. But look around—the Thandrid have been coming at these people. Hard. We're coming into this at the end. They had time, and they lost it. This is a final move."

"Yeah," Star-Lord said. "I'm getting that. I just . . ."

"What?"

"I just really didn't like seeing those things take you down yesterday," he said, looking ahead as they walked. "That's all. I just . . . it didn't look good. Can't get it out of my head."

"I'm fine," she said, an edge of defensiveness to her voice. When he looked up, open concern on his face, she knew she'd misread him. It was still instinctual to take everyone's doubt as an insult to her honor as a warrior, but that wasn't what this was. She lowered her voice and repeated her words, this time softly. "I'm fine, Peter. Really."

He nodded. "Okay. Stay that way."

"I will."

"Promise?"

"I promise."

"I'll be so mad if you die," Star-Lord said.

"Peter."

"So mad. You don't even know."

As planned, by the time they were in view of the crash site, the two Thandrid war crafts had passed overhead, moving toward the second front of rebels. Gamora noticed Jesair look over her shoulder at the departing craft with a deep sadness in her eye. Though it went unspoken, Gamora knew that the Rebel Queen, along with her people, accepted that there would be losses this day. They could've shot down the ships from a distance, as they had yesterday, but instead, the Incarnadinians needed to lure the crafts away from the site, close enough to engage in a firefight. Indeed, as the Guardians, Jesair, and the eight rebels settled into their hiding space as the Thandrid pickup craft began to land next to the two crashed ships, they heard an exchange of shots in the distance.

The craft, the same as the sleek white ships seen on Spiralite, landed with fluid grace, blue light flashing from its sides as it descended. Once it had touched down, an opening on the top slid back with a hiss and the first of the lanky creatures climbed out, the colorful light from Incarnadine's rings shining off of its gleaming, black exoskeleton. Within moments, three more Thandrid exited the craft and approached the destroyed ships.

Star-Lord raised his quad blaster, but Gamora cleared her throat.

With everyone looking toward her, she pulled four throwing knives from her belt. "Save your ammunition and power," she whispered. "I'll collect these once they've done the job."

"May I?" Jesair asked, holding out a gloved hand.

Gamora nodded and mouthed a silent affirmation. She placed two of the knives in Jesair's hand, and then turned back to the Thandrid.

"Wait until their breathing lines up," Jesair said. "If we miss even one, we have a fight on our hands—and that's assuming we don't have more Thandrid in the ship, waiting. If we pick the exact right moment . . . we drop them with a single pop."

"Just from experience back on Bojai, I'll add that we should wait a few moments after the pop, just to see if more Thandrid emerge from the ship," Gamora said, watching the Thandrid's faces open and shut from their vantage point. The knife was cold in her hands. "We don't want a nasty surprise when we walk up."

"I *said* I was sorry about that!" Rocket snapped. "Will you torture me forever?"

"We already forgave you, Rocket," Gamora said, closing one eye as she positioned the knife.

"Oh," Rocket said. "That, uh, that wasn't about me."

"Nope."

Gamora and Jesair tensed as the Thandrid breathing began

to line up as they drew nearer to the craft. The two warriors shared a look, and then turned back to their enemies, who crept below, unaware of the hidden assassins that lay in wait.

"Annnnd . . ." Gamora whispered. The Thandrid's faces finally all shut at once. "Now!"

She and Jesair tossed the knives. They moved through the sky, Gamora's in a twirling arc and Jesair's in a straight line. All at once, they hit their homes, each of them instantly piercing the Thandrid air-sacs. The sound of the four popping at once was a single crack, cutting through the silence and then echoing through the open air like applause.

Gamora looked over at Jesair, nodding in approval. "I would've never tried the lunging throw. Interesting."

"My mother taught me," Jesair said.

"Sounds like my kind of woman," Star-Lord muttered.

After waiting for a few short moments to be sure no stray Thandrid were coming out of the pickup ship to check on their fallen buddies, the team made their way across the field. Stepping over the Thandrid bodies, Gamora looked back in the direction of the other two ships. They were still in the sky, lighting up the ground below with blazing blue energy beams. She imagined that makeshift pub full of smiling and laughing Incarnadinians the night before, and knew that, at this very moment, some of them were taking their last breaths. They'd clung to life until the end, and then charged into a battle this morning, knowing full well what might happen.

As Gamora approached the Thandrid craft, surrounded by those she loved most in the universe as well as new but trusted allies, she thought of the Bojaians, who had been deluded into thinking that they were suffering from some kind of plague. By the time they knew that they were being taken over by the Thandrid, if they ever did, it was too late. They were dying without even being given the chance to know what was at risk, without being given the chance to fight.

Gamora hadn't been able to look Star-Lord in the eye when she'd promised that she'd survive, because the truth was, she couldn't know. But as the Incarnadinian guard boarded the Thandrid ship, followed by Jesair and Drax, then Groot and Rocket, and then Star-Lord, who looked back at Gamora and stretched out his hand, Gamora was grateful that she was given the same chance as those Incarnadinians.

The chance to face her enemy and fight for her life. It might not have been an enviable position by most estimations, but it was better than some got.

CHAPTER TWELVE

Flying in a Line

Rocket

"I say this as someone whose bunk smells like sweaty feet and old dipping sauce," Rocket said, poking the squishy, organic walls of the ship's interior with the tip of his claw. Fluid rose from the porous surface, collecting on his claw tip in a drop of black paint. "This is one nasty ship."

He cringed, wiping the liquid off on his pants as the Guardians and rebels, their weapons at the ready, searched the ship for any stowaway Thandrid or other threats. Its foul stench was the first thing Rocket had noticed, but was by no means the only thing about the ship that made his already deep distaste for the Thandrid intensify. While the exterior was sleek and white, as sterile as Z'Drut's fortress back on Spiralite, the interior was lined with fleshy walls that exuded hot, moist air, and pulsated every few seconds like the slow throb of a weakening heartbeat. The ship had no seating, no engine access, and no bunks or other rooms—it was simply an open space, lit by a wide cylinder of blue Spiraline light that protruded from the ceiling. In the center of the ship was the control panel, a simple projection device that was currently displaying a two-dimensional image of Incarnadine's geography, digitally marked with various symbols.

Rocket believed, from the way that Jesair glared at the image, that the symbols signified fallen territories. Or, even worse, perhaps future targets.

"Are we good here?" Star-Lord asked. "If we're gonna try this thing, we better try to break atmo before those warships come back and see their buddies' balloons popped."

"I think that's a 'no' on any hidey holes," Rocket said, shrugging. "Think we got all of 'em."

"We?" Gamora asked, sharing a grin with Jesair.

Groot eyed the walls of the ship suspiciously. "I am Groot . . ."

"Indeed. This tissue does appear to be *alive*," Jesair said. "I'm not reading any signs of communication coming off of this substance, though, so I think we can safely conclude that the ship isn't sentient."

"What's the difference?" Rocket asked.

"A tree is alive," Jesair said. "Groot is sentient. Both can feel, but only one can act with purpose of its own accord."

Rocket waved his paw dismissively, trudging over to the control area. "As long as it's not gonna spit one of those buggy bastards out at us, I don't care. Let's go ahead and see if we can figure out how to get this sludge bucket moving."

"You should write a book of poetry someday," Star-Lord said. "Put that talent of yours to good use."

Rocket ignored him, swiping his paw along the screen. The projection disappeared, which he took as a good sign. If he was able to pull up the map of the larger solar system and then focus in on Spiralite, that meant that the ship operated in a similar way to the *Milano*—and that, he could fly any day.

The screen remained blank, though, and no further projections came up as Rocket attempted to program the touch screen. He tried a few different methods, but nothing seemed to work. In fact, nothing happened at all for the first few moments until, gradually, he began to notice that his fur was prickling with static, beginning to stand on end. As he looked at the raised hair on his paws, the screen before him blinked out. Black.

"Oh, no you don't!" Rocket snapped and looked under the panel, attempting to locate a wiring system. Nothing. The screen was plugged right into the ship's energy core, tapping into that potent Spiraline energy that didn't seem to want to work for him. *Too bad,* he thought.

Everyone's eyes were on Rocket as he attempted to reactivate the black screen. He felt the air fill with tension. Drax had started to grind his teeth, which he did whenever he was impatient—a sound that drove Rocket crazy even when they were just hanging out over dinner or drinks, but which was worse now that everyone in the ship was waiting on Rocket.

Taking a deep breath, attempting to remain patient, Rocket looked down at the deactivated control panel, trying to remember if he'd ever seen a ship act like this. He knew that, with perseverance, a calm mind, and careful thought, he could figure it out.

Drax's teeth squeaked as he continued to grind them.

Rocket let out a guttural scream, lifting his tiny fists over the panel. "YOU DON'T WANNA WORK?" Rocket snarled. "I'LL SHOW YA WHO'S BOSS!"

Just as he was about to smash his fists down on the panel, he felt roots wrap around his wrists. Groot pulled the thrashing Rocket up from where he stood by his arms, and proceeded to place him down at a safe distance away from the machinery.

"I am Groot," Groot scolded.

Rocket pointed at Drax. "He's grinding again! You hear that crap? He's grinding like a madman!"

"Look!" Drax blurted, throwing back his head for a hearty laugh. "Everyone laugh at his fur! He looks ridiculous! And cuddly!"

Rocket, amidst a few scattered chuckles and Drax's barking laugh, looked down at his body. Indeed, not only the fur on his arms, but all of the thick, grey hair that covered his body was standing on end, making him appear far fluffier than tolerable. Rocket, his eyes going white, lunged for Drax, but Groot was there to stop him. He pulled Rocket back again, and Drax laughed even harder.

"Are you guys serious?" Star-Lord said. "We have to go if we're gonna go! Rocket, if you can't figure out the ship, no need to go all puffy. Let me have a look."

"Wait," Gamora said, narrowing her eyes. She strode over to the panel, and waved her hand over it. She walked over to Rocket and Groot, showing them the hair on her arm, standing on end. "Static."

"Kinda thought that was obvious!" Rocket snapped.

"Didn't you feel that same thing when the Thandrid communicated telepathically?" Gamora asked. She pointed to the base of her skull. "Right here?"

"Yeah?" Rocket said. "So what?"

"*So* . . . I would wager that the ship is waiting for Thandrid communication," Gamora said gravely. "I don't think we're going to be able to fly it. Not alone at least."

Jesair closed her eyes slowly. "You mean . . ."

"Yes," Gamora said. "We would need a hostage."

"Wait . . ." Rocket said, narrowing his eyes.

"Dude, we know you're gonna punch the thing if we let you back over there," Star-Lord said. "I'm with you on the hostage thing, Gamora. Maybe we could—"

"No, I mean it! I think I have an idea. Hear me out on this one," Rocket said. He walked away from Groot over to Jesair, eyeing her up and down. "Last night, Groot wouldn't shut up about what *you* were saying to him. About how most folks see speech existing in a lineup."

"Existing in a *line*," Jesair said.

"If you can talk and understand things outside of that, uh—that line, right? Couldn't you interpret the Thandrid speech?" Rocket asked. "Couldn't you feel out what the ship is trying to say?"

Jesair furrowed her brow. "I've never attempted to communicate with a ship before. We don't know the function of the organic material within this craft, so I'm not sure if I'd know where to begin. I feel that it feeds off the Spiraline energy, but beyond that . . ."

"You said it's alive, didn't ya?" Rocket asked.

"Yes, but not *sentient*."

"Well, we're about to not be alive or sentient ourselves when those walkin' cockroaches come back and find us hanging around in their ship!" Rocket snapped. "Don't you think you could try?"

Jesair closed her eyes and then, slowly, a wide smile spread across her face. "Yes. Yes, I can."

Rocket extended his arms, directing Jesair over to the controls. She walked up to the black panel and stood there, slowly raising her hands until they were within the warm field of static. She moved her fingers, as if she was tracing invisible shapes in the air.

"*Oh*," she said, her smile widening. "Ohhhhh."

No sooner did Rocket feel that familiar, creeping buzz of static in the base of his skull did the panel light up with a bright flash of blue. The 2-D map formed from the light in front of Jesair, first showing that same image of Incarnadine's ruined cityscapes and then, as Jesair's smile fell, the view pulled out into a distant view of the solar system, including a swath of glowing dots that formed a seemingly endless barrier—the drones' force field.

"I knew it!" Rocket cried. "I'm a freakin' genius!"

"*Jesair* is the one who did the work," Drax said, grinning proudly.

"What, you got a crush on her, lover boy?" Rocket asked with a laugh. "It was my idea, you teeth-grindin'—"

"I would never attempt to crush Jesair!" Drax roared. "Watch your tongue, or you will find it removed and nailed to this unpleasantly moist living wall! Which is not sentient!"

"You two are ridiculous," Gamora said, coming between them. "Rocket, your idea was good. Calm down. And Drax, yes, Jesair is indeed the one who did the work. How about we stop yelling loud enough for everyone on the planet to hear us and let Jesair concentrate?"

Rocket nodded, glaring at Drax. "Yeah. Fine. But meathead over here better watch it. I'm still brassed off about that fluffy comment, so I gotta warn you—I'm a bomb of nasty, just waiting to blow! Give me a reason, Drax. Give me a reason."

Drax shrugged. "You were fluffy, though."

Rocket clenched his teeth.

In front of the control panel, Jesair's lips moved quickly

and silently, and the map began to shift. It zeroed in on Spiralite, moving closer and closer until the energy tower itself came into view. Its blue flame moved on the screen, glowing bright enough to light the entire ship.

"There," she said with a smile, and suddenly, the ship jolted.

"Ha-ha! Here we go!" Rocket cheered as the ship began to shake. He held out a paw to Drax, who looked down at him through narrowed eyes. Then, he let out a deep, throaty laugh and smacked Rocket's paw. Rocket let out a victorious yelp and jumped up and down, all of his anger relieved. So what if he was fluffy? They were moving, and he was thrilled.

As they began their journey from the war-torn Incarnadine to the Thandrid base of Spiralite, the others began to discuss their plan of attack. Drax, however, motioned for Rocket to break away from the crowd. Once they were across the ship from the others, Drax lowered himself to his knee, gesturing for Rocket to lean in.

"'*Crush*,'" Drax said. "This means a . . . feeling of love?"

"Sometimes love, sometimes a tingle in the pants," Rocket said. "Wait a sec, is this . . . you're feeling pants-tingly for Jesair? I was just messing with you! I had no idea, you big studly hunk of muscle!"

"There is no tingle," Drax said. "Perhaps a stirring in my heart."

"A 'stirring in your . . . ' Who even are you?" Rocket said.

"Hey, you know what? If she has you talking like *this*, go for it. Please. This is hilarious."

"I tell you this as to excuse my behavior," Drax said. "I am . . . defensive of her honor. I apologize for threatening to nail your tongue to this disgusting wall."

"You know what? Bygones. Let's take this tower down, fix Bojai, get our money, not die, and then you can sweep your rebel queen off of her feet," Rocket said. "Which, just to get ahead of you—that means *impress* her."

Rocket and Drax returned to the group, and began to solidify their plans. Rocket knew his role. Once they'd slowed down enough and were within range, he'd pop out of the ship with the Y.G.A.F.P.S.Y.W.P.O.F. 6000 and let off a few good shots at the tower. If the drone walls fell, they'd know—and they'd get out of there without looking back, hopefully avoiding a direct exchange of fire. If the drone wall *didn't* come down, they'd hit Z'Drut's fortress with a Y.G.A.F.P.S.Y.W.P.O.F. 6000 blast and make their way back to Incarnadine to regroup. Star-Lord seemed wary of the plan, as did Groot and a few of the rebels. Rocket didn't want to think about possible failure though. He would do his part come what may. He had his friends and his weapons—from where he stood, no one in the wide and edgeless universe could stand up to that.

"Whoa!" Star-Lord said, breaking from the group. He walked over to Jesair, motioning for the rest of the Guardians and the rebels to gather around. Jesair was staring at the glowing blue map, perplexed. The holographic projection showed a mass of odd shapes congregated on the other side of the drone wall.

"What's that?" Rocket asked. "Looks like a bunch of moons popped up out of nowhere."

"No. This isn't just a map," Gamora said. "It's a live feed."

"Wait a second . . . Are those *ships*?" Rocket asked, pointing at the projections. Indeed, the objects were moving along the wall, as if searching for a break in its force field. "Looks like they're trying to get in. Should we warn 'em?"

"Can we?" one of the Incarnadinian rebels asked.

"No," Jesair said, circling her hand over the shapes. The map shifted closer to them. "If anyone could get in . . . it is the Nova Corps."

Indeed, with a bow of Jesair's head, the glowing blue projection zoomed in on the shapes until they were clearer. Now, Rocket could see the red star of the Nova Corps emblazoned on the ships. There were five of them, each ten times the size of the *Milano*, gathered in formation outside of the drone wall. Peppered all along the impenetrable wall of energy were floating shuttles, presumably full of soldiers examining the force field in hopes of breaking through.

"They're right here," Rocket said, marveling at the ships. "So close. Just at the edge of the system. Unbelievable."

"If a crew like *that* can't get in . . ." Star-Lord said, trailing off.

"Now is most certainly not the time to despair," Gamora said. "We already knew the drones couldn't be stopped from the outside. The plan doesn't change. We attack the tower."

"And if it doesn't work?" Rocket asked. "Then what?"

"I am Groot," Groot said solemnly.

Star-Lord looked toward Rocket and Jesair. "What did he say?"

Rocket unhooked the Y.G.A.F.P.S.Y.W.P.O.F. 6000 from his back strap, hoisting it into his grasp. Once it was positioned on his shoulder, he kissed his paw and then smacked the tip of the barrel.

"He said 'Then we fight,'" Rocket said. "Which, I don't know about you jokers . . . but either way, I'm looking forward to blowing some crap to pieces."

They flew until the congregation of Nova Corps ships was no longer in view on the map. As they prepared to land on Spiralite, all of their anxious banter gave way to a heavy silence. Spiralite's landscapes completely filled the screen as they entered the atmosphere, beginning the final descent toward the energy tower and the army of Thandrid that guarded Emperor Z'Drut's stronghold. Rocket closed his eyes, feeling the weight of his weapon on his shoulder, and braced himself for their landing.

CHAPTER THIRTEEN

Valley Low

Drax

The tense silence unnerved Drax as they descended closer to Spiralite, flying over the vastly unpopulated cities and farmland. Drax's eyes were trained on the holographic projection, which showed them a far vaster view of the planet than they'd seen when they were initially taken in and forcibly docked by the drones. In the lands they were passing there weren't many Thandrid—nor much of anything else. Drax noticed a few congregations of beings that looked similar to Z'Drut, small and catlike, but they fled for cover when they looked up and saw the passing Thandrid ships. When the second group they passed hid as they soared above, Drax looked up to meet Gamora's eye.

They both knew what this meant.

They continued through Spiralite, uninterrupted as they headed toward the capital city. Drax noticed, though, that even tranquil, unshakable Jesair was rigid as she stood before the glowing projection of Z'Drut's energy tower, piloting the ship with intense concentration. She seemed as if she was prepared to react in an instant if they were shot at by the ground forces below.

No such thing happened, though. Their flight progressed smoothly until they began to arc down toward the tower for their final descent. Their plan from here on in was simple: when they reached shooting range, Jesair would use the Thandrid ship controls to pepper the tower with attacks as they circled around for a landing, scattering the Thandrid guard that surrounded the tower. And then, upon landing next to what would hopefully be the unprotected tower, Rocket would emerge from the ship with the big gun and blast it with his weapon that, as far as Drax was concerned, would remain nameless.

They would know right away if the attack was successful— with the Nova Corps right outside of the drone wall, its obliteration would allow them instant access to Spiralite. All the Guardians had to do was avoid a midair onslaught from the other Thandrid ships until the cavalry showed up.

As their ship crossed over the land on which the prison, Z'Drut's fortress, and the energy tower were located, a flash of bright blue light burst from their screen. Jesair gritted her teeth and held her hands in front of her as if she was cradling a sphere. She turned her hands in a circular motion, and the ship tilted momentarily to the side, curving in a deep arc. On the screen, a glowing projectile shot past their ship and exploded in the sky.

"What was that?" Rocket barked.

"Exactly what we were hoping to avoid," Star-Lord said.

"We've been discovered. The Thandrid are firing from below," Drax said, walking up to Jesair, who leaned closer to the control panel. All around them, the Guardians and the rebels prepared their weapons, knowing that this was about to turn from an offensive strike to a defensive mission. "Can we shoot the tower from here, Rebel Queen?"

"No," Jesair said, but closed her eyes, a vein pulsing across her temple as she concentrated. The ship lurched forward as it sped up, making a dash for the tower. "We must be closer."

"Then closer we will get," Drax said, lifting a fist. "They wish to shoot us from these skies, which only serves to stoke the fires of my rage. We will advance, and we will triumph! The tower will fall, the drones will fall, and then—then, THE CLAM-FACES WILL FALL! Each of their sacs will pop, as we, the Guardians of the Galaxy and the great rebels of brave Incarnadine will claim our victory! We—"

By the time Drax heard the sound behind him, it was too late to act. It was a moist ripping sound, like a powerful liquid adhesive ripping off of something fleshy. Confused, Drax turned his head to peer over his shoulder, but the black tendrils were too quick. They lashed out from the organic wall and wrapped around Jesair.

"Foul creature!" Drax snarled, leaping for Jesair.

The wall had come alive all around them, reaching for the

Guardians' weapons, and, worse, dragging their pilot away from the panel.

"Release the mighty Rebel Queen!" Drax bellowed. She reached for him, but the tendrils tugged her out of his grasp with a powerful jerking motion. Drax threw himself forward in bounds, until he was upon the wall, ripping his fingers into the base of its tendrils.

As he wrestled with the slick, slimy limbs attempting to pull Jesair into the wall, the ship took an immediate, sharp turn down.

"Grab on to something!" Star-Lord shouted. "Not the tentacles!"

"There's nothing BUT tentacles!" Rocket snapped right before he was sent toppling away as the ship turned on its side. Groot reached for him, but ended up turning over and skidding across the floor himself, knocking a few panicked Incarnadinian rebels down. The ship was spinning out of control, and everywhere he looked, Drax saw one of his friends either being choked by the living walls of the ship, which had clearly responded to the alarm on Spiralite, or skidding across the floor.

"Release us, foul living ship!" Drax shouted. "We will show no mercy on your vile flesh if you harm a single Incarnadinian!"

Drax gritted his teeth as the ship picked up speed, spinning out of control. His friends slid all over the floor, as the

Incarnadinians attempted to climb across the deck to get to the control panel. He did not know if they had Jesair's skill, but he *did* know if someone didn't take control soon, they would crash.

Digging his fingers into the tendrils wrapped around Jesair, he blocked out everything else. *She* was the only one who could fly the ship, thus the first who needed saving. Drax ripped at the tentacles that flowed up Jesair's face, blocking her mouth and covering eyes. They resisted, sticking to her flesh stubbornly until Drax twisted and pulled even harder, peeling them off of her with an awful, wet sound. As the tendrils were removed from her lips, Jesair gasped in air, coughing and sputtering as Drax threw the limp, withering alien flesh to the side.

"My deepest gratitude," she said, her white hair ruffled. Drax fought the urge to touch it by turning back to the wall, just in time for more tendrils to shoot toward her. Drax intercepted them, grabbing their sticky, gelatinous flesh in his hands. The ship dipped again, and, together, they were thrown forward. They spilled across the ground, toward the control panel. Drax reached out a hand as they tumbled, grabbing the panel. He held on tightly, and pulled Jesair up toward it.

"Go! I will hold you still so you don't fall," Drax said. "You can right this ship's course, Rebel Queen, before we—"

Drax's words were cut off by a terrible crash, as the ship, still at full speed, clipped something solid. Cold air burst in around them, and Drax's vision became a tumbling blur of inky black tendrils, Groot's branches, rebels, and weapons as the ship flipped out of control. A second and final crash sent the craft skidding along solid ground, ripping open the bottom with a series of harsh scraping sounds. Drax instinctually reached out for something to grab, something to right himself so he wasn't toppling out of control. He found a hand.

The ship came to a stop after four harsh bounces. Drax saw, in front of him, Jesair, gripping his hand, her white eyes wide as they stood on the ceiling of their overturned ship. She wasn't looking back at him, though. She was staring at the tear in the ship's hull. The damage seemed to have killed the organic security system, which drooped all over the ship in steaming, liquefying puddles of noxious black gunk.

But the ship wasn't the only casualty.

An Incarnadinian rebel, a fresh-faced young man with lavender hair and eyes that looked like moonstones, was pinned to the side of the ship by a lip of metal that jutted out from the inside, stabbing through his back and coming out his chest. Jesair slipped out of Drax's grasp and walked over to the rebel, who bled blue from the wound and his mouth. He was still breathing, his body shaking with every weak, airy gasp. The Guardians and remaining rebels stood, watching as Jesair stroked the dying rebel's hair three times, until he took his last breath in her arms.

Drax knew that they had no time for this, that there would be something terrible waiting for them on the outside . . . but he didn't say anything. Didn't question Jesair. He remembered her words about how no one Incarnadinian was seen as above or better than any other. He wondered if that was only regarding social ranks, or if it applied to love as well. He wondered what love meant if everyone was seen as equally important by everyone—if it cheapened the idea of love, or if it made it all that much deeper. He wondered if, with every rebel lost, Jesair lost her husband all over again.

Without a word, Jesair strode back over to the control panel. Now that the ship had been capsized, it was above them all like a glowing, digital chandelier—but still, even though the organic material of the ship had perished, the energy instantly responded to her, filling the room with that static once more. The map expanded before their eyes, and they saw where they were.

Rocket let off a string of curses.

"Yeah," Star-Lord said. "I gotta second that. We're *not* close to the tower. Not by a long shot."

"What did we crash into?" Gamora asked.

"The prison. I believe . . ." Jesair said, and then paused, narrowing her eyes. "That sound . . ."

Drax grabbed his twin blades from his belt, flipping them in his hands. He heard the exact same thing she did: a thunderous roar from outside, building and expanding like an approaching wave. It was a crowd, that much could be sure. And they were screaming, but not in pain.

"A battle cry," Drax said. "Enemies approach."

"Maybe," Gamora said. "Thandrid don't make noise, though."

"Wait a second," Rocket said. "I know what that is! I've heard that sweet sound a few times in my life, and I gotta say . . . there's nothing quite like it."

"What are you talking about?" Star-Lord asked.

"Open the door," Rocket said. "Take a look for yourself."

"I believe Rocket speaks the truth," Jesair said with a smile. "How odd . . . that in a fatal fall, we find grace."

Drax furrowed his brow, thoroughly confused. "Grace?"

Jesair waved her hand up toward the panel, and the ship split open. All around them, they saw various races of aliens— Spiralines, Badoons, Aakon, Epsiloni, and countless more—flooding out of the ruined structure that had been the prison. The entire west wing had been taken out, leaving a huge opening that had unleashed a horde of prisoners from within. Thandrid were all around, armed with metallic guns that shot blue beams of Spiraline energy at the prisoners, but there were too many of them. The Thandrid guard were being overwhelmed.

"I don't know if I'd call it *grace,* exactly . . ." Rocket said, stepping out of the Thandrid craft with his huge weapon balanced precariously over his shoulder. "It looks more like an old-fashioned, sac-poppin', fascist-slayin' prison riot to me."

CHAPTER FOURTEEN

An Old-Fashioned, Sac-Poppin', Fascist-Slayin' Prison Riot

Star-Lord

"Rocket, hold on," Star-Lord said, grabbing his friend by the shoulder before he could step out into the midst of the riot taking place not more than a hundred yards away from the craft. Drax was standing by the tear in the hull with his knives, ready to ward off any of the rioters who may have mistaken them for Thandrid aggressors because of their ship. "We need you and your big honkin' gun intact when you get to the tower. Let's hold up a sec. Our big plan just kinda went to hell, so we need to strategize."

"I run to the tower. I shoot the crap out of the tower," Rocket said, ripping free from Star-Lord's grip. "You guys cover me!"

"I mean, yeah, okay. I don't think that's enough, though. We can't bet on just one option now," Star-Lord said, snatching him up by the collar.

He looked around at the others gathered in the ship, settling on the seven remaining rebels. After watching one of them die in Jesair's arms, it was like he was seeing them for the first time.

When Star-Lord and his friends arrived on Incarnadine, it seemed that they'd found the solar system's last stronghold of warriors. Battle-worn survivors. The last chance at taking Z'Drut and the Thandrid down. And they were all that, yes, but now, suddenly, Star-Lord looked at them—*really* looked at them—and saw something else. He saw fear, and excitement, and hope, and even a little bit of bloodthirst. He saw that some of them were very young. It was easy to look at a group of soldiers, especially when they looked different from him, and see them as a collective instead of as individual people—but Star-Lord knew that his next words might determine which of them lived and which . . . well, the other thing. That weighed heavily on him, now that he had taken the time to look from face to face.

But he had to say it anyway.

He took a deep breath and continued. "I think we have to spread the fighting out a bit. I'm not saying I want any of us to go off on our own—their numbers here are crazy big. We can't mess with them on that front. But I'm thinking this prison break is going to have a biiiig load of Thandrid flocking this way. Like I said, we can't bet on just one option; it's a long way to the tower, and if we charge, we're still outnumbered—so if we fall, that means we *all* fall."

"We must attack from multiple angles, then," Drax said.

"Exactly. Both literally and figuratively. I'm good with Rocket's assault on the tower as Plan A, but we need to be working on a B and a C while he makes his way over," Star-Lord said. "Gamora, you made it up to Z'Drut's office, right? Think you could get us in?"

"It was heavily guarded," Gamora said. "But, then, I've got an equally heavy grudge against these bastards."

"Figured you might," Star-Lord said. "That's you and me. I think we could do it with three of your team, Jesair, judging by the badass weaponry and general devil-may-care-type attitudes I'm seeing."

Jesair nodded to the rebels. "Coldios, Boret, Jujuine." Three of the rebels broke off and walked over to Star-Lord, who held out his fist to them.

"Ah," the oldest of the three, a female rebel with a missing eye and scars down her cheek said with a smile, inclining her head. This was Jujuine. "I am to momentarily embrace this with my own knuckles."

She tapped Star-Lord's fist with her own, and then Coldios and Boret followed.

"Awesome," Star-Lord said. "I doubt Z'Drut would allow the Thandrid to have complete and exclusive access to his tower anyway. While you guys try to blast the tower to pieces, we'll put the pressure on Z'Drut. If he has a fail-safe to bring those drones down, we'll make him spill."

"Who's gonna watch my back?" Rocket asked.

"That's where Groot comes in," Star-Lord said.

"I am Groot," Groot said, hoisting up Rocket onto his shoulder.

"Exactly, dude," Star-Lord said, flashing him a thumbs up. "Do that leg-growy thing, haul bark over to the tower, and Rocket—light 'er up."

"Ka-boom," Rocket said, grinning viciously.

"Drax and Jesair—I'm thinking you and the rest of the rebels could keep the riot going while looking out for Rocket. Spread out, and make sure they're safe," Star-Lord said.

"That's an A and B," Gamora said. "What's Plan C?"

Star-Lord shrugged. "I'm thinking maybe pass out weapons to all the prisoners who don't look super evil? You know the type, Drax."

"Yes," Drax said. "I will arm only the good, morally grey, and moderately evil."

"Tell 'em there's, like, buried treasure under the tower or something," Star-Lord said. "If all else fails, maybe they'll . . . uh . . . knock it down themselves?"

Drax narrowed his eyes and Gamora cringed as some of the rebels shifted uncomfortably.

"What?" Star-Lord said. "I didn't say it was a *good* plan. It's a Plan C! Plan Cs are a stretch at best. I've heard worse Plan Cs."

"May I interject?" Jesair stepped forward. "I said back on Incarnadine that it would be best for you to formulate a plan if things went awry here, as they indeed have . . . but I do have a suggestion."

"Hit me," Star-Lord said.

Drax raised his fist, preparing to punch Star-Lord, but then caught himself, narrowing his eyes. He then nodded silently, and held up a fist. "You wish to be assaulted, not with fists, but with information. Proceed to slap him in his face with your ideas, Jesair."

"I can still operate this ship," Jesair said. "The crash killed the organic defense system, but I can feel its telekinetic pull functioning at one hundred percent. Once you've gotten off the craft, I can take to the air and keep you all safe from above as Rocket and Groot journey toward the tower. I can, perhaps, even continue the plan and knock it down. That might be our Plan C."

"So the buried treasure thing is Plan D," Star-Lord said.

"Why don't we just go ahead and *all* stay in here then?" Gamora asked. "If the ship is working, why risk leaving?"

"The ship is no longer physically stable, despite its system still functioning," Jesair said. "If I pilot it alone, I can fly close enough to the ground to not endanger myself, but attempting to fly with a larger crew would be far too risky. I don't believe that its firepower will be enough to take down the entire tower, but if we can damage it enough to make the drones falter, perhaps the Nova Corps will be able to exploit that. And, failing that . . . I can fly the craft into the tower. We clipped the prison, and you saw what that did."

"You will not have to make such a sacrifice, noble as it is," Drax said. "You are mighty, and you will succeed."

Jesair took Drax's hand and offered him a soft smile. "I appreciate your confidence, Drax. I will do what I can."

"Okay, shifting buried treasure to Plan E, then," Star-Lord said, clapping his hands together. "Let's do this!"

Groot

Star-Lord nodded solemnly to Groot, who knew what that gesture meant. At once, it said "good luck" and "hurry up." Groot wasn't entirely sure about how much luck he generally had, especially given the events of the last day, but *hurry up*? That, he could do.

Groot, with Rocket on his shoulders, ducked out of the Thandrid craft and stepped into the yard in the midst of the prison riot. Right before them, two Thandrid guards were taking down a burly alien whose entire face was just an eye. The alien fought back, slamming his open eye into the creatures' exoskeletons, but he had been separated from the main area of the riot and was being overpowered by the two insectoids.

Groot's shadow fell over the Thandrid as they wrestled the prisoner to the ground.

"I AM GROOT!" Groot roared, stabbing his arms through their faces until his branches popped the air-sacs. The Thandrid dropped, sliding off of Groot's arms with a dry scrape, and the cyclops prisoner looked up at them in fear.

"Hey! You evil?" Rocket asked.

"Wouldn't go far as to say all that," the cyclops said, dusting himself off. He then began to stomp the Thandrid's corpses until their exoskeletons cracked.

Rocket peered down at Groot, who shrugged.

"Take one of these!" Rocket said, shaking his hip forward. A modest pistol went skittering across the floor to the cyclops, who looked at it with a gleam in his eye.

"Thanks, vermin!" he replied and snatched the gun up, already running toward the next Thandrid guard as Rocket began to shout curses after him.

"I am Groot!" Groot said, and began to advance toward the energy tower, passing by the gaping hole in the empty structure that had been Spiralite's prison. All around, prisoners were fighting guards, but in the distance, around both the tower and Z'Drut's fortress, a large swarm of the looming Thandrid approached. Groot felt the roots within his chest tighten as they had when he saw his friends overwhelmed by the creatures back on Bojai, but this time was even more frightening—the Guardians of the Galaxy weren't together, and the Thandrid had weapons.

"Go, go, go you big lug!" Rocket cried, fumbling with his paws to snap his Y.G.A.F.P.S.Y.W.P.O.F. 6000 back into place on his back. "Gah—I should've waited to whip this thing out.

The pose looked so cool, but we need some heat of the more immediate variety."

With Rocket struggling on his back, Groot took sweeping steps through the prison yard and headed straight toward the tower, which lit up the sky with its blazing blue light in the distance. He launched himself in a single stride over the open flames in the prison yard's pit, where prisoners were attempting to force Thandrid guards to fall into the blazing furnace. He elongated his legs, his roots extending with every step, increasing his leg span by twofold . . . four . . . six. The Thandrid craft in which they'd landed was in the distance now, and, as Groot took long, reaching steps to avoid Thandrid breaking away from the prison riot to attack him, he resisted the urge to look back and see how his friends were doing. If he kept running across that open field, avoiding the skirmishes between the guards and the prisoners, and beating the incoming hordes of Thandrid, he could make it.

Maybe.

"Just . . . one . . ." Rocket groaned, fumbling with his oversized weapon.

Right then, a chunk of wood-like flesh exploded on Groot's thigh. A swarm of eight Thandrid, holding out their glowing guns, rushed at them from under the swell of a grassy hill, shooting a stream of blue lasers their way. Groot felt the burn of the attack, but pushed his flesh to grow back as another shot went through his shoulder.

"Hell with the smaller crap!" Rocket cried, lifting the Y.G.A.F.P.S.Y.W.P.O.F. 6000 high once more. "EVERYONE WHO DOESN'T LOOK LIKE A BUG, START RUNNING!"

"I am Groot!" Groot shouted as two more shots sent splinters flying from his side. "*I am Groot!*"

"Nah! To hell with that!" Rocket said. "I got enough ammo! They're lighting us up! Can't have that!"

Rocket cranked the gun back despite Groot's continued protests, and let off a wicked shot. A white-hot fireball blazed out of the gun's barrel, hurtling toward the incoming Thandrid. They began to scatter, but it was too late. The fireball detonated as it slammed into the ground, shaking the area so badly that Groot lost his footing.

They went careening down, just as a second swarm of Thandrid came at them from the side. Groot scrambled to get up, the acrid smell of burning exoskeleton filling his nostrils as flames spread across the grass to the side.

The Thandrid were on them, their numbers even greater than the first group. Groot stood, using one hand to hold Rocket in place, but one of the Thandrid took a running leap toward Groot, barreling right into his legs. Groot fell again, and this time, Rocket tumbled off of his shoulders.

Fumbling to aim the Y.G.A.F.P.S.Y.W.P.O.F. 6000 on the ground as the Thandrid came down on him, Rocket let out a furious battle cry.

Groot reached for him, but one of the Thandrid got there

first. He opened his face with a wet, throaty hiss and then clamped it down on Rocket's gun.

"I AM GROOT!" Groot cried, as he heard the metal of the gun whine under the Thandrid's pressure.

"Are you crazy?" Rocket cried, pulling on the weapon as the Thandrid bit deeper into it. It began to spark, letting out a high-pitched whistle. "We need the Y.G.A.F.P.S.Y.W.P.O.F. 6000!"

Groot felt a Thandrid latch onto his back and begin shooting him at close range, but he had more immediate worries. Rocket's gun was about to explode, and the little guy was too stubborn to realize it as he wrestled to free it from the Thandrid's mouth.

"I . . ." Groot said wrapping his roots around both the clamped Thandrid and the Y.G.A.F.P.S.Y.W.P.O.F. 6000, which now let off a wicked heat that scalded Groot's flesh.

"Groot, no!" Rocket cried.

". . . AM . . ." Groot bellowed, wrenching the Thandrid, the Y.G.A.F.P.S.Y.W.P.O.F. 6000 still in its mouth, away from Rocket.

"What are you doing?" Rocket yelled. "My Y.G.A.F.P—"

"GROOT!" Groot roared, flinging the alien and the weapon into the thick of the masses of oncoming Thandrid. Rocket's weapon hit the ground with a horrific explosion that stretched fifty feet into the sky, and then another smaller explosion that burst from the ground, sending chunks of charred exoskeleton raining down on the field. Their entire field of vision lit up with blinding afterglow, and the heat was immediate.

Rocket climbed up Groot's bark, settling in on his shoulder. " . . . Oh."

Now, with no weapon big enough to take down the whole tower, Groot nevertheless ran toward their destination again. He hoped that Jesair had taken to the skies, and that she would see the wide patch of fire. She would understand what had happened, Groot hoped, and would aim immediately for the tower.

As they stepped over a disembodied Thandrid claw, Rocket clung tightly to Groot with one paw, going through his weapons with the other.

"What are we gonna do?" Rocket asked. "I don't got anything else nearly that nasty. Not blow-the-building nasty, anyway . . ."

"I am Groot," Groot said, pushing on.

"Yeah," Rocket said. "Well, we'd *better* figure something out."

Gamora

Despite the fact that Rocket had confidently called it a riot, from where Gamora stood, it was very clearly a war.

Along with Star-Lord and the Incarnadinian rebels Coldios, Boret, and Jujuine, Gamora pressed through the Thandrid forces that formed a blockade between their assault and Z'Drut's fortress. While her allies were taking Thandrid down with well-timed shots, Gamora was once again using her blade on the ground, cleaving through her enemies' clamped faces with renewed energy. She wasn't going down again like she had last time. The swarm of Thandrid was mounting around them in all directions the closer they got to the door, but Gamora refused to retreat. She knew what their numbers meant.

Emperor Z'Drut was in there.

She hooked her arm around a Thandrid's face as it charged her and then launched her feet up in the air. She wrapped her legs around another Thandrid's face and, using her momentum, twisted her thighs, sending them both to the ground. As they hit with a bone-grinding crunch, the Thandrid faces opened with two gasping breaths, exposing their air-sacs to the flash of her blade.

Gamora pressed on, within a few yards of the door, Star-Lord by her side.

"We're gonna make it in!" he cheered. Gamora saw blood running from a gash in his head, and she hoped he wasn't delirious.

"You good?" she asked.

"Oh, yeah," he said. "This is my favorite thing, almost dying. Wish we did it more often. Never get enough."

The three rebels, sticking close to Star-Lord, shot down the Thandrid in front of the pristine, white facility. Where the prison was a crude, stone building and the tower looked like a five-hundred-foot tall, bony limb reaching for the sky, Z'Drut's facility was short, low to the ground, much like the emperor himself. Gamora wondered if that was purposeful—that the deceptive ruler operated out of a building that appeared small to the common observer, but ramped down into a deeper, darker area once you got inside.

Gamora pushed closer to the rebels and saw that Boret was hurt badly, a pool of blood forming below him with every step he took. Within a yard of the facility now, she grabbed the Thandrid nearest Boret and smashed her boot into its chest. It slammed against the shut, white doors with a sharp clatter.

Gamora gritted her teeth and jammed her blade into the Thandrid between her and the door, running forward with her blade, her elbows locked. All around, Thandrid shot at them, but the Incarnadinian rebels had formed a cover around her, deflecting the enemy attacks with their own handheld shields. The fire came from everywhere, though, and blue blood sprayed into the air.

Gamora gave her blade a final, powerful push into the Thandrid's face. Its air-sac popped and she kicked it away, slamming its back into the door. Star-Lord, stepping in front of her, obliterated a chunk of the door with a shot from his quad blaster. As they stepped through, the rest of the ruined door fell to the ground outside with a clatter, knocking one of the advancing Thandrid in the head.

Jujuine and Coldios backed into the facility along with Star-Lord and Gamora, who was once again blinded by its bright white walls and glowing blue light. The Thandrid collectively hissed from outside, already pushing forward to follow them inside, despite the rebel's continued shots.

Boret was nowhere to be seen.

Jujuine looked at Gamora over her shoulder as she held her ground in the threshold. "There will be more in here. Coldios and I will hold this area as best we can. Find Emperor Z'Drut."

Gamora and Star-Lord shared a look, knowing what this meant. Gamora also knew that she didn't have time to question them. Giving Coldios and Jujuine a nod, she grabbed Star-Lord's arm and pulled him along with her in the direction that the Thandrid had taken her earlier.

"They're gonna die," Star-Lord said, his voice thick.

"We're the only ones who know where we're going," Gamora said.

"I know that," Star-Lord said quietly. "It's just . . ." he trailed off, his voice thick.

Gamora nodded, looking at him through the side of her eye. She felt a rush of compassion for him. "Yeah. I know."

They advanced down the ramping, monotonously white hallway that the Thandrid had taken Gamora along one day earlier. It grew quieter with every step they took.

Gamora held her blade tightly as they took the turn toward the hall that would lead to Z'Drut's office. Suddenly, as they stepped into that final stretch, their field of vision filled with Thandrid, all of them already letting off blinding shots of blue energy.

"They were waiting for us!" Star-Lord said as he flicked his wrist and sent up a holoshield device, which covered them at the last minute. The device floated in midair, shimmering as it blocked the shots, but the Thandrid kept on firing as they got closer.

Gamora looked at the Thandrid, trying to count them. Fifteen. Maybe twenty.

"On three, snatch the holoshield out of the air," Gamora said. "Hit them with it, and then we shoot and slice until we're through. You with me?"

"You know I am."

"Don't use that 'we're going to die' tone on me, Peter," Gamora snapped.

"Right. Totally gonna live. You and me. One hundred percent surviving the impossibly overwhelming odds."

"One," Gamora began. "Two . . ."

Drax

Drax, speckled with blood both his own and others', looked to the sky from the middle of the battlefield that had once been a prison yard. He let out a barking laugh as the Guardians' stolen Thandrid craft took to the skies, soaring over the rioting prisoners below. He continued to laugh as he stabbed both of his blades simultaneously into a Thandrid guard's air-sac.

Another Thandrid, creeping toward him from the side, shot Drax in his burly neck with a ray of Spiraline power that grazed his flesh. Drax didn't stop laughing at he turned on his attacker, slicing his blades outward. All around him, the prisoners, their numbers larger than Drax could've ever known from what they'd seen the day before, fought back against their captors.

Drax landed a kick squarely into the Thandrid's face, sending it stumbling back toward the fire pit. He'd seen others sending Thandrid to fiery deaths, and would rather enjoy the chance to do so himself.

"Gaze at the skies and tremble with fear, clam-faced oppressor!" Drax said, headbutting the Thandrid toward the flames. It resisted, pressing back against Drax, but the burly warrior was rejuvenated by watching the craft, piloted by Jesair, blast the crowds of Thandrid from above as it glided toward the energy tower. It struggled, weaving and dipping as it advanced, but it seemed to be moving toward its goal.

With another laugh, Drax leapt in the air and launched a double-kick at the Thandrid's chest, sending him stumbling down into the pit, right into the open flame. All around, prisoners cheered as the creature thrashed in the flame, which quickly devoured it with a burst of foul gas. Finally, the Thandrid came to a stop, and its face burst open in time for its air-sac to swell and pop, revealing a mounting fire in the depths of its skull.

Drax climbed to his feet and pounded on his chest. "You are lucky to burn! The Rebel Queen Jesair rains down hellfire on you! No clam-face will be safe from her revenge!"

"Did . . . did you say Jesair?"

Drax turned around to see the source of the trembling voice. A male Incarnadinian, his skin marred by healed scars as well as fresh wounds, stood before Drax, weakened from what appeared to be many brutal sessions of torture. In the distance, the fight waged on between the prisoners and the Thandrid, but this Incarnadinian prisoner looked at Drax with hope in his eyes.

"Yes," Drax said. "Your queen. She will be pleased to hear that one of her own people survived the Thandrid imprisonment."

"My queen . . ." the Incarnadinian said, a smile touching his face. He looked at Drax, and tilted his head to the side. "I can see her in you. Her kindness has touched you. I am glad."

Drax narrowed his eyes, taking a closer step to the prisoner.

"Who is Jesair to you?" Drax asked.

The Incarnadinian looked up at him through shining eyes. His skin had lost much of its luster, and he was painted with blood both dried and new, but despite his injuries, he stood strong.

"She is my wife."

Drax's eyes widened. "You are the king."

"I was," the Incarnadinian said. "And, if Jesair lives as you say . . . by the grace of fate, then yes . . . I still am."

Drax sighed deeply, looking back up at Jesair's craft. "Well . . . balls."

CHAPTER FIFTEEN

Where Have All the Spiralines Gone?

Star-Lord

"DUCK!" Star-Lord said, throwing himself in front of Gamora as he flicked a laser grenade into the crowd of remaining Thandrid.

He and Gamora hit the ground together as the hall lit up with the blast. Star-Lord covered his head while chunks of exoskeleton rained down on them. Not wanting to pause to give any of the survivors a moment to recuperate, Star-Lord jumped to his feet.

A single Thandrid remained standing, its half-deflated air-sac hanging out of its ruined face. It took a shaky step toward Star-Lord and, behind him, Gamora readied her blade. There was no need, though. Before it could manage another step, the creature fell face first on the pile of Thandrid parts, the final burst of air escaping its sac in a weak puff.

"That was a *pffft*!" Star-Lord said. "That was totally a *pffft*. Can't wait to tell Drax."

Gamora brushed his hair off. "You're singed."

"Yeah, I'm surprised I'm not faceless," Star-Lord said. "That was like . . . way too close to throw a grenade. I got kinda last-resorty there for a sec."

"I don't blame you," Gamora said. "These things are nasty."

Star-Lord looked ahead to Z'Drut's door. There were symbols that Star-Lord didn't recognize etched into its surface.

"I saw these earlier," Gamora said, tracing her fingers along the sliding panel. "I tried to remember which lit up when the Thandrid opened it, but it was too quick. I think they opened it telepathically."

"Damn," Star-Lord said. "You don't think we could force it?"

Gamora stuck her blade into the lip of the door and pulled. She squeezed her fingertips in, her muscles rippling as she attempted to force the door open. Star-Lord joined her in her efforts, but the doors didn't budge.

"Stuck," she said. "We'll need to grab a Thandrid. If we can get one alone, maybe we can force it to think the door open."

"We could do that," Star-Lord said, reaching for his belt. He pulled out another grenade, tossing into the air like a baseball. "Or . . ."

Gamora

One explosion later, Gamora was walking through the ruined husks that had been Z'Drut's sliding doors. She wouldn't admit this to Star-Lord, but she had given a bothersome amount of thought to the symbols, trying to recreate the light pattern she'd seen when the Thandrid had first entered. That was one thing she appreciated about the Guardians of the Galaxy, though: she could always count on Star-Lord, Groot, Rocket, and Drax to cut corners in the most brilliantly ridiculous ways.

"Imagine that grenade blast just killed him. He did look pretty freakin' fragile. Like, he's in here, packing up his stuff to make a run for it, and boom! Grenade busts open his door, he trips, bangs his squishy little head. Good night, emperor," Star-Lord said as he followed Gamora into the room.

"Better hope not," Gamora said. "We need that little slimeball."

Star-Lord blinked repeatedly, which served to confirm another theory that Gamora had been playing with. He shielded his eyes, looking around the room. "God, it's tacky in here. What is this, some kind of visual torture? Man, oh man."

"Something like that," Gamora said. When she'd learned, beyond a shadow of a doubt, that Z'Drut had aligned himself with the Thandrid in an attempt to dominate his solar system, she had begun to look back on their meeting, dissecting every interaction in hopes of divining a greater meaning. More than anything, she remembered the way that, after walking through a purely white, sterile building, the rush of clashing colors in his office took her off guard. It reminded her of something that Thanos used to do—he never mentioned it, but Gamora had taken notice. When taking a meeting, whether it be with an ally or an enemy, he would often increase the lighting in his throne room so it was blinding. From the start of the meeting, the other party would be taken off guard, and thus susceptible to Thanos in an entirely different way. As an adult, Gamora knew exactly what that was: signal interruption. Introduce a familiar circumstance to create expectation, and then gain the upper hand by subverting that expectation. It was deceptive and small minded, Gamora thought.

But effective.

Star-Lord, his eyes scrunched up, looked around the room as Gamora stood silently, forcing her eyes to adjust.

"Come out, Z'Drut," Gamora snapped.

"Yeah," Star-Lord said, rubbing his eyes. "Show yourself, you little—"

The crackling sound of electricity interrupted Star-Lord, who fell to his knees. Blue bolts flowed over his body as he convulsed, taken off guard by the prod that stuck in his ribs. Gamora lifted her blade and looked to see that a long pole extended from Star-Lord's side to all the way across the ground . . . beginning under the ruined shell of the door. She brought her sword down on the prod, which popped with a spark of blue power.

She kicked aside the husk of the door, revealing Emperor Z'Drut on the other end of the broken pole. He stared at Gamora with fury in his eyes.

"And there we are," Gamora said.

His chest rose and fell as he gathered himself up, facing off against her. "How *nice* to see you," he hissed.

"I . . . I'm good," Star-Lord said, standing, holding a hand to his side. His face was red and his chin was slick with spittle, but he walked in place, shaking his limbs. "Whew. Ow. Totally fine."

Gamora rushed forward and grabbed Z'Drut by the neck. She hoisted him up and then pitched him across the room. With a satisfying crack, he slammed into his desk, falling to a crumple at its foot.

"Be careful," Star-Lord said, wiping his face. "Remember. He's Plan B."

"He's something else, too," she said. She stood over him, pointing her blade at his throat. "Fascist."

"Call me what you would like," Emperor Z'Drut said. "If the single survivor of a race condemns me for my actions, how can I take insult? Clearly, your way is no better. Where are your people, Gamora? Has your way led to anyone's salvation?"

"Dude," Star-Lord said. "You might want to not insult the badass lady who is holding a sword to that pencil you call a neck. Just saying. Also, still *ow*."

"Your *people*? Is that who you're attempting to protect? Interesting," Gamora said, pushing the flat surface of the blade against his throat. "Where are they?"

"Alive, because of *me*," Z'Drut said.

"Aside from the thousands of Thandrid in this city, the planet is nearly empty," Gamora said. "The surviving Spira-lines flee when they see a Thandrid craft. They don't hold your fondness for the species. Tell the truth. I want to hear you say it."

Z'Drut glared at Gamora. "A daughter of Thanos calls *me* a fascist. Accuses *me* of genocide. How . . . interesting. If I die with this final thought on my mind, at least it amuses me."

Gamora lowered her blade. "You're not going to die today. Not if you work with us. You have to answer for what you've done, but we will spare your life."

"If?" Z'Drut said.

"If you disable the drone wall," Gamora said. "Now. With-out another word."

Z'Drut raised his eyebrows, smiling calmly. "It cannot be done from here. And, before you carry on with whatever physical threats you have to offer, that is not a lie. There is a single location that can shut down the power source being fed into the drones, and no, I do *not* have that in my personal quarters."

Star-Lord and Gamora shared a look.

"The tower," Star-Lord said. "We were right."

Z'Drut narrowed his eyes. "You assume much."

"Call it an educated guess," Gamora said. "Your prison has been destroyed. Your facility, invaded. Next up is that tower."

Z'Drut opened his mouth to say something, but his lips just quivered as the sound caught in his throat.

"And there it is!" Star-Lord said. "Energy tower confirmed. Thanks, little guy."

Z'Drut held up his hands, his expression deflating. "I acquiesce. Take me where you will. But do *not* . . . under any circumstances . . . think that any of us will survive that tower's destruction. It will take out the entire city with it. More."

Gamora narrowed her eyes. "What do you mean?"

"The amount of raw energy harnessed within those walls is enough to power a galaxy," Z'Drut said. "Attempting to blast it down will incinerate all life within conceivable proximity, if not the entire planet."

"You're lying," Star-Lord said.

Z'Drut stared at him expressionlessly. "Perhaps."

Gamora took Z'Drut by the back of his neck with one hand, her blade at the ready in the other. "Move. We're heading to the tower. If you're so scared of it blowing, then we'll do it your way. We'll turn it off. Together."

"Try to take me all the way across this land," Z'Drut said. "If we make it as far as the prison yard, I'll crown you both emperors of Spiralite."

"I really wish we could just waste this guy," Star-Lord said under his breath.

Together, they walked into the hall, Star-Lord and Gamora flanking the captured emperor. Their boots crushed Thandrid exoskeleton as they advanced up the ramping, curving path. It was the only sound. Before they had entered Z'Drut's chamber, the facility had echoed with the sounds of battle between the rebels and the Thandrid in the entry way. Now, it was quiet.

"Be ready," Gamora said.

Star-Lord pulled out his quad blaster, rolling his shoulders. "You bet."

"Even if the drone wall falls . . ." Z'Drut said. "The Thandrid—"

"Oh, shut up," Star-Lord snapped.

"No," Gamora said, pushing Z'Drut forward. "Let him talk. The Thandrid *what*?"

"They've accomplished their goal. Bojai teems with their spawn. Incarnadine has become nothing but pockets of resistance. There are *billions*. Shortly, the Thandrid empire will eclipse that of the Skrulls and the Kree."

"And where does that leave the Spiralines?" Gamora asked.

"I did what I could to help . . ." Z'Drut said. "You must understand, this was the only way. Under the Thandrid empire, I will be given a new planet to begin Spiralite once again, with the survivors of my kind . . ."

"Who, the ones who didn't resist when you sold your planet out to killer bugs?" Star-Lord snapped.

"There were casualties, yes. But my people had already been decimated. Those who resisted stood against the only way *any* could survive. I mourn their deaths, but I welcome that loss if it means we avoid extinction. This time, with the protection of the Thandrid from the start, we can start over. In this new order, Spiralite will be untouchable, and the Thandrid will thrive. Take down my planet. Take down the wall. You cannot stop what is already done."

Star-Lord kicked Z'Drut in the small of his back, sending him sprawling forward. "Are you waiting for me to say that genocide is chill as long as you mean well? Gotta say, we're not gonna agree on this topic, little guy."

They turned the corner and found the entryway littered with Thandrid bodies. Gamora scanned the area for Cold-ios and Jujuine, or any remains, but couldn't spot them. She didn't dare hope that was a good sign, though. The Thandrid bodies were piled high, as had been the odds—it had been scores against two. The Incarnadinians were powerful and resilient, but the Thandrid were legion.

"Ah," Z'Drut said as they crossed the threshold. "I admit, I believed you wouldn't get this far. I was certain my guard would have held even to my threshold. I can only commend you."

"Shut up," Gamora said.

"Just one more thing," Z'Drut said. He held Gamora's gaze for a minute, a sense of peace falling over him as his lips curled up into a vicious smile. "*Implode.*"

The moment the word left his mouth, the building shook violently, the ground rumbling below their feet. Bright, blue flames ripped out of the walls behind them as the fortress reacted to Z'Drut's command. The ground beneath Gamora split, and she had to throw herself forward to avoid falling into the sudden rift. The blue energy burst out of the walls like a series of bombs behind them, each explosion sending a horrible tremor through the battlefield.

Z'Drut took the opportunity to rip himself free of Gamora's grasp. Star-Lord lunged for him, but the threshold blew to pieces, cutting his face as he attempted to snatch the little emperor. Star-Lord, his face bleeding, stepped forward, but his foot caught in a crack in the ground. Gamora, her heart pounding in her chest, grabbed Star-Lord by the arm as Z'Drut ran away. She pulled Star-Lord out of the threshold, supporting him with her shoulders as they barreled forward onto the field outside.

Thandrid soldiers were already marching toward them as Z'Drut sprinted away from them in the direction of the energy tower.

"He's going to the tower," Gamora said as Star-Lord wiped the blood off of his face. "Why in the world would he go toward the tower?"

Star-Lord didn't have the time to answer Gamora's question. As the facility continued to implode behind them, the Thandrid soldiers were on them. Gamora sliced at them, trying to regain her focus, but she knew that they were too close to the facility. She needed to drive the Thandrid back and get distance—but Z'Drut was also escaping.

She barreled into a Thandrid, pushing it back toward the field. The ground shook.

"Peter!" Gamora shouted. "Follow him!"

"Hell no!" Star-Lord said, taking down a Thandrid with his quad blaster. "We're not splitting up. Not now."

"I know!" Gamora said. "Don't be an idiot, I've got these! Chase him down, make sure he doesn't disappear. I want to focus on staying *alive* for a moment, and then I'll catch up."

The ground shook with another explosion.

"You remember," Star-Lord said, sending a few more shots at the Thandrid. Five of them remained. "You promised."

"I do," Gamora said, rolling away from an attacking Thandrid. Now, with space, she began to run backward, leading the Thandrid away from the exploding fortress. "And remember—don't kill him!"

Star-Lord gave her one final worried look and then sprinted after Z'Drut. Gamora stood, gripping her blade tightly as the five remaining Thandrid soldiers lifted their pistols at her.

She grinned. "Go on. Try me. I haven't popped enough of you cockroaches yet today."

Rocket

"Yeah! Take that, ya freaks!" Rocket yelled from his spot on Groot's shoulders, launching laser clusters at the Thandrid's faces, watching them convulse and then pop. He and Groot had been stuck in place a few dozen yards from the energy tower for what seemed like forever, shooting and striking down the endless flood of Thandrid coming at them. The Thandrid seemed to be focusing all efforts on keeping Rocket and Groot away from the tower. That, to Rocket, meant they were in the exact right place, no matter how much of his fur was being charred by the laser blasts shooting past from every angle.

Which was a *lot* of fur.

As Rocket continued to return fire, Groot pointed to the sky. Rocket saw Jesair's ship moving slowly toward them from the corner of his eye, but looked right back to the Thandrid, lighting them up with more fire.

"What, Groot?" Rocket asked. "Kinda got my hands full here!"

"I am Groot!" Groot called, and this time, Rocket turned to see what his friend meant. He was right—Jesair's stolen ship was faltering as Thandrid shot at it from below. It was dipping lower and lower, until it became close enough for a few of the Thandrid to leap onto it and grasp the hole in the side of the hull.

But Rocket saw something even more disturbing back toward the fortress.

Groot took a lurching step toward the ship, but Rocket pulled on his leaves, stopping him. "Groot, wait!" Rocket said.

"I am Groot!"

"I know Jesair's in there!" Rocket said, pointing beyond the ship. "But *look*!"

Emperor Z'Drut was running full tilt toward the tower, pursued by Star-Lord a few yards behind him—alone. Rocket's mind instantly began to race. He pictured Gamora laid out on the battlefield somewhere, bleeding out. He gritted his teeth and, bending his knees, launched himself off of Groot's shoulder.

"I've got Jesair," Rocket said as he landed on the ground, launching a deadly shot at a Thandrid barreling toward Star-Lord. "Help Star-Lord! He's ground-bound—I think he needs a lift!"

"I am Groot!" Groot bellowed in affirmation as the Thandrid collectively turned their attention toward Star-Lord.

Emperor Z'Drut, his speed increasing with every step, ran directly toward an entrance a few hundred yards away from where Rocket and Groot were trying to get in. The Thandrid guards parted and the sliding doors opened with a burst of blue energy and closed immediately behind him. The Thandrid then closed ranks, blocking Star-Lord as he ran closer, not stopping.

Rocket forced himself to focus so that Groot could do his thing. He turned away from the hellish scene and toward the ship that was being overrun by hissing, slashing Thandrid.

Groot
Crushing as many Thandrid as he could as he walked on his elongated legs toward Star-Lord, Groot fought through the

pain of the lasers blasting his hide to pieces. He bent toward Star-Lord and knit the roots of his arms together, forming a basket of branches for his friend to step into.

"Whoa!" Star-Lord said. "Thanks man! My rockets are totally busted. Got shot to hell by the Thandrid back there."

Groot, kicking off the Thandrid scaling his body as they figured out what he was doing, forced his way over to the tower. He held Star-Lord out to its surface, just a yard away. Star-Lord held out his quad blaster and sent shot after shot into the tower, until a hole formed in its siding. Groot held Star-Lord with one hand, feeling his legs begin to give way as the Thandrid below ripped at him. He reached for the hole to steady himself.

"I am Groot!" Groot bellowed as he dug his roots into the tower, ripping the siding off. His leg broke below from the Thandrid attacks, but he forced his other hand up, bringing Star-Lord right up to the hole.

"You're the man, Groot," Star-Lord said, climbing into the tower. "Keep kicking butt down here, dude. I'm gonna end this."

"I am Groot!" Groot called to Star-Lord before turning around to face the Thandrid horde. He dropped to his knees, regrowing his feet as laser blasts flew at him. The Thandrid began to flood into the tower, but Groot knew he'd given Star-Lord some space to operate.

Groot saw Rocket running toward where Jesair's ship had finally been pulled down into a horde of Thandrid. Neither

Drax nor Gamora were in sight. The Incarnadinian rebels were gone. Groot looked up at the tower into which Star-Lord had disappeared and, as Thandrid scaled Groot's body, forcing him down to the ground, he couldn't be sure if any of their many plans had worked, or if any of it made a difference at all, but as his vision filled with gleaming exoskeleton and slashing, wet blades, he closed his eyes, lashed out his branches, and hoped.

Drax

"There!" Drax shouted, pointing ahead at the fallen ship. He had seen it go down moments before, as he had been gathering a group of prisoners to storm the energy tower. Panic burst in his chest as he saw the Thandrid overcome the ship and he'd been running toward it ever since, with his small group of followers behind him.

He, the Incarnadinian king, the rebels, and a group of prisoners descended on the group of Thandrid that was fighting Rocket on the surface of the ship. The air filled with the sounds of their popping air-sacs as the two factions clashed. Rocket climbed up onto a confused prisoner's shoulders and began to shoot the Thandrid, allowing Drax to make his way through the crowd, tossing Thandrid aside, not even reacting to the shots of lasers cutting through his skin.

He pushed his way into the ship, leaping on the only surviving Thandrid on the inside. Using his weight, he pulled the

Thandrid down. Its face slammed against the control panel, which burst in a rush of blue energy. The Thandrid kept its face clamped shut until Drax smashed it over and over against the hot, jagged remains of the panel. At last, its face opened with a dry hiss and Drax slammed it into the broken controls once more, a final pop echoing through the ship.

Drax glanced around, panic swelling in his chest. He didn't see her.

But then, he heard her. "Irn . . ."

Drax turned and watched Jesair pull herself out from under the pile of Thandrid corpses. Irn, her husband, climbed into the hole in the ship, his body trembling as he got nearer to her. He threw his arms around her and, for a moment, as they embraced, openly weeping, Drax felt the instinct to look away. But he fought it, watching them hold each other. When Jesair opened her eyes, and Drax saw the bewildered, impossible happiness on her face in that moment, he felt a sudden lightness of being. A smile spread across his lips and, for a moment, he allowed himself the fantasy of seeing his own wife, and his precious children, somehow alive after he'd spent years thinking they were dead. He imagined the feeling, the unfathomable relief, that unknowable grace, and, in seeing Jesair overcome with the power of that very emotion that he could never feel, Drax felt a sense of peace deeper than he knew possible.

He waited patiently as Jesair and Irn stood. The sounds of the battle outside quieted, except for Rocket's manic laughter, which told Drax that they were no longer in immediate danger. The Thandrid, after all, were flocking in droves toward the tower. That was where the real danger was.

Jesair looked from Irn, to Drax. "How?"

"They kept me alive . . . near the brink of death . . ." Irn said, stroking her hair. "Every day, they'd attempt to break into my mind. To force me to reveal something about our world . . . I don't know if they were able to divine anything from my thoughts, but I fought. I fought with everything I had. With all of the prisoners, though, and all of the bodies . . . so many bodies . . . I was certain you'd been killed, Jesair."

"I was certain that *you* had been killed," Jesair said, choking back a sob. She turned to Drax, her eyes shining brightly. "My Drax. Thank you. My gratitude for your deeds exists beyond words. We have pushed this city to war, and many are dead. You've kept my king safe. My soul grows at the thought of your bravery."

Drax nodded. "I understand . . . as does mine."

"Not to break up the tender moment in here," Rocket called, "but we've got a tower to charge!"

Drax, Jesair, and Irn climbed out of the hole in the ship, joining Rocket, the rebels, and the prisoners. In the background, Groot stood by the tower with large chunks missing from his body but his legs elongated, beckoning them to join him as he smashed two Thandrid together, over and over. He was bellowing "I am Groot! I am Groot!"

"What's he saying?" Drax asked.

"Well, he thought we were all dead, so he's pretty happy," Rocket said. "Also, Star-Lord made it into the tower. We have to get up there, now."

"Star-Lord is in there alone?" Drax said. "What of Gamora?"

Rocket looked down, gritting his teeth. "I haven't seen her."

"And Coldios? Jujuine? Boret?" Jesair asked.

The silence hung in the air, answering her question. She closed her eyes, grasping Irn's hand.

Drax shook his head. "No. I do not accept this. This is a large field, with many warriors—but none so cunning, none so swift, none so powerful as Gamora! Except maybe me. But Gamora lives . . . and if she does, I have hope for the others."

"Never been big on hope, myself."

Drax, along with the others, looked in the direction of the familiar voice. Gamora stood, with Coldios and Jujuine behind her. They were worse for the wear, each of them sporting deep cuts and laser burns—and worse for Jujuine, whose one functioning eye had been turned into a bloody mass. Coldios held her up as he bled from his own deep gash on his collarbone.

"Gamora!" Rocket said, running toward her. He hugged her legs.

"I'm sorry," Gamora said, looking toward Jesair. "Boret didn't make it."

Jesair and Irn breathed the information in, accepting it

with great sadness. Drax was in awe of Jesair, but now Irn as well. He found it easy to pair Jesair's love of all and boundless kindness with her beauty, but he now sensed the same in the hobbling, injured figure of Irn. He found himself, in spite of the odds, smiling once again.

"Z'Drut let it slip," Gamora said. "We were right. We shut down the tower, we bring down the drones."

"Hell, yeah," Rocket said. "Ka-BOOM!"

"No," Gamora said. "Z'Drut . . . and I don't know if he was lying, but we can't take a chance . . . he said that if we were to blow it up, the amount of energy released would destroy us all. We have to work our way into the tower and turn the power off, somehow."

"Then that is exactly what we will do," Drax said. "Let us march on the clam-faces one final time. For those who have fallen . . . and for those who will live this day. We fight!"

As Drax led the march forward, running toward Groot and the tower, he heard Rocket whisper, "Did Drax just give a semirousing speech? Am I dead? Is this some weird afterlife where nothing makes sense?"

Drax grinned, gripping his blades. He wasn't sure if Rocket spoke literally, but he agreed with part of it. Very little made sense in life, but, amazingly, Drax was beginning to see that there was, if not order, a certain poetry to it all.

With that thought in mind, he led his friends and allies toward the tower for their final stand against the Thandrid.

CHAPTER SIXTEEN

High on Believing

Star-Lord

Star-Lord had been walking through the dark, metallic laby-rinth of stairs and bridges that made up the energy tower for long enough to feel that he might have been searching in the wrong area. His initial thought was that whatever source was emanating the energy connected to the drones was high up in the tower, so he'd been climbing, but there were no Thandrid guarding this area, which was more than a little suspect.

If I was an evil alien warlord, Star-Lord thought, *I would have, like, a hundred guards all around that area.*

Just as Star-Lord went to turn back, he stopped himself. He furrowed his brow, unable to shake the thought he'd just had.

Emperor Z'Drut was nothing like him. Nothing like the normal alien warlords Star-Lord had encountered in the past.

Z'Drut had had every chance to kill or imprison the Guard-ians when they first came to his planet. Instead, he found out what their business was on Bojai and, seemingly concluding that they were no threat, allowed them to leave. Instead of draw-ing possible Nova Corps attention by attempting to kill a team as well known as the Guardians, he let the circumstance work itself out. Perhaps he hoped they'd make the drop on Bojai, arrange for payment, and leave, never even noticing the situation on Bojai. Had Kairmi Har not been infected, that is exactly what might have happened. Or, maybe he expected them to die on Bojai—better than having it happen on his planet, at least.

Whatever Z'Drut's intentions were, Star-Lord didn't care. His original intention might not have been to kill the Guardians of the Galaxy, but he had devastated three planets in attempting to secure his own survival. He didn't think like normal people. Even in the simplest move, such as the placement of guards, he was playing chess. Not checkers.

Star-Lord sighed, knowing that he could be overthinking a simple matter, but nevertheless turned back around. He jogged up the next set of stairs, picking up speed.

"Oh, if I'm right about this, I'm so smart," Star-Lord said. He hurried down the corridor, glancing around the bend. Looking up, he saw that the next set of stairs led to a short bridge connected to a set of two doors. At the end of the bridge above him, he saw a Thandrid leaning over what looked like a jukebox with a holographic 2-D projector screen similar to the one in their stolen ship. There was nothing else above the bridge but the opening at the top of the tower, which was placed right above the jukebox. The box itself was shooting out a thick, concentrated beam of blue energy, so dense that it was no longer bright.

"I *am* so smart," Star-Lord said to himself as he slowly moved up the stairs, his quad blaster ready. Taking each step gingerly, as not to alert the sole Thandrid to his presence, Star-Lord crept up. He was suddenly glad they hadn't bombed the tower. Judging by the looks of the energy that jukebox was giving off, the force of it suddenly stopping might have taken out the whole planet. He'd need to shut it down, somehow.

When he got to the bridge, he stepped in front of the two doors as quietly as he could. He knew full well that behind said doors could be a room filled with more Thandrid, but in this moment, the current Thandrid operating the jukebox was still facing away from him . . . an opportunity that Star-Lord was going to use to his advantage.

He pointed the quad blaster at the Thandrid's hips, hoping the shot would spin the creature around so he would get a better shot at its air-sac. He took his first step off of the metal of the stairs and onto the bridge . . .

Which creaked.

The Thandrid spun around, hissing in surprise, its air-sac inflating.

"Aw, thanks!" Star-Lord said, bringing up his quad blaster to face level. He let out a single shot—normally, it would've been two, but the amount of energy coming from the controls was unnerving. The Thandrid closed its face in time to protect the air-sac, which Star-Lord didn't expect. The blast hit its head, scorching its exoskeleton, but not killing it. The

213

Thandrid rushed toward Star-Lord, who wished, for the first time in a long time, that he had Gamora's skills with a throwing knife. He bet she could throw one right in that partition while the thing moved and pop its sac like a balloon.

He hoped she was okay.

Star-Lord, not wanting to let off another shot so close to the energy, threw himself to the floor of the bridge. The Thandrid, startled, tripped over him. It reached to grab his face, its hard and dry skin scraping Star-Lord's head. Blades ripped out of its forearm as it prepared to stab Star-Lord, pulling back his head to expose the flesh of his neck.

Star-Lord blocked the Thandrid's attack with his quad blaster, not letting off another shot, but catching its arm-blades in the lower grip of his weapon. Now that the gun was pointed down, at the Thandrid and away from the energy, he let off four simultaneous shots. The collective blast took out a chunk of the Thandrid's face. Cringing, as the Thandrid thrashed in his grip, Star-Lord plunged his hand into the creature's face and felt the rubbery, moist texture of its air-sac.

Pop.

Star-Lord, breathing heavily, stood, shaking the foul mucous off of his hand. "Yep," he said to himself. "About as gross as I imagined."

He looked over his shoulder at the doors behind him. No Thandrid forces flooded toward him, and that pop had been particularly loud with the echoing acoustics of the tower's pinnacle. Star-Lord was sure he was alone now.

He walked up to the jukebox, his hands positioned over it at the ready when the dread set in. It *was* the same type of projection screen technology from the ship, which no one he was aware of besides Thandrid or Incarnadinians could fly. The odds that he'd be able to fight his way *out* of the tower, pair up with an Incarnadinian, fight their way back up, and make it all the way to the controls without being killed were laughable. He began to touch the screen, squinting at it. There had to be *some* way. There was no way that Z'Drut would *only* trust Thandrid with operating the very energy that had made his planet a target to begin with. Star-Lord was sure there was a way around. There had to be.

Before he could put another thought to it, though, he felt a sudden hot snap in his left leg. It gave way under him, and he stumbled, almost falling face first into the deadly beam of concentrated energy the jukebox was projecting. He grabbed for the machine, but slipped, falling to the floor.

He looked up to see Emperor Z'Drut stepping over the dead Thandrid, a pistol powered by Spiraline energy glowing brightly in his hand. One of the doors in the distance was open behind him.

The pistol was trained directly on Star-Lord's head.

"Hello, Peter Quill," Z'Drut said calmly. "Please believe me when I say that I respect you for getting this far. I'd hoped that you would go on about your business and leave my solar system with your ineffectual medication left on the *nest* formerly known as Bojai, but unfortunately, you had to pry. Thankfully, you haven't done any irreparable damage."

Star-Lord stared up at Z'Drut, pain shooting up his leg. He gritted his teeth, his mind racing.

"Trust me when I say that, as much as you may hate me, I did not initially intend to kill you . . . but now, I've been left with no other recourse. I'm sure, if you could stand where I do and look out at a planet with a history like my own, you'd look at the man before you and pull the trigger as well," Z'Drut said. "As a show of respect, I intend for you a quick death. A death worthy of a man who has, until now, matched my every move. Or, perhaps a fool that has stumbled into dumb luck. In any case—"

Star-Lord began to convulse at Z'Drut's feet. He shook violently, letting out strained, guttural sounds, his body contorting and tensing. The bridge rattled as he continued to seize in front of Z'Drut. His teeth chattered and spittle foamed out of his mouth as he convulsed, slamming his body over and over onto the metal of the bridge . . . until he stopped, falling still.

Z'Drut, perplexed, took a step forward and peered down at Star-Lord, his eyes narrowed. He let out an airy laugh. "Felled by a shot to the leg? Unbelievable."

Star-Lord then whipped his leg up in a wide arc, kicking

Z'Drut's hand. His boot connected with the pistol, freeing it from the stunned alien's grip. Star-Lord broke into action, lunging forward and wrapping his arm around the emperor's neck in a headlock. Z'Drut looked at Star-Lord, not comprehending what had happened, as the grinning Guardian of the Galaxy squeezed the alien's neck without mercy.

The pistol clattered down the long chamber of the tower, banging against multiple flights of stairs before disappearing from sight.

"Nah," Star-Lord said, using the back of his hand to wipe the spittle from his chin. "What's unbelievable is that you fell for *that*. I mean, come on. If you shoot a guy and he starts to have a seizure, you don't go '*Huh, how did that happen?*' You shoot him again! Are you serious, bro?"

Z'Drut let out a strangled howl from within Star-Lord's grasp.

"What was that, little guy?" Star-Lord asked, dragging him over to the controls.

"You . . . buffoon!" Z'Drut choked out. "You clown! There is no honor in flopping around at your enemy's feet like an animal."

"You're the one who said I'm all respectable and stuff," Star-Lord said. "Come on, sing it with me, my guy: *R-E-S-P-E-C-T!* Know what it means to me? Totally nothing, dude. You're a fascist who sold out his own planet and allies for freaky bugs."

"You haven't won," Z'Drut croaked.

"Not yet," Star-Lord said. He grabbed Z'Drut's hand. "But I'm thinking I'm about to."

Z'Drut tried to wrench his hand from Star-Lord's grip, but Star-Lord just tightened the headlock.

"Yep," Star-Lord said. "Exactly what I thought. You'd never let those things have full control over the energy, huh? What happens if you give the jukebox a high five?"

"Give the *what* a *what*?" Z'Drut rasped.

Star-Lord grinned. "You'll see."

He forced Z'Drut's hand onto the panel. They stood there for a moment, watching as the beam of energy continued to send power up into the sky. Star-Lord's grin faltered as the screen didn't react.

Then, after a moment of holding Z'Drut there, the screen's glow began to falter. Star-Lord let out a triumphant *"Woo-hoo!"* as it flickered to black and the holographic projection of the drones began to blink out one by one.

"Awwwww yeah, punk," Star-Lord said. "You know what that means. It's raining drones! Hallelujah, it's raining drones!"

Z'Drut squirmed in Star-Lord's grip, but it was too late. One by one, the drones went dark until the hologram itself blinked out.

Then, above it, the beam of Spiraline energy began to dissipate as well, becoming wisps of light, bright-blue power, until it was completely gone.

Star-Lord looked down at Z'Drut. "Hey, how's that for

permanent damage? Rate me on a scale of one to ten. Be honest. I can take it."

Z'Drut didn't respond this time. He went limp in the crook of Star-Lord's arm, defeated.

"I'll take that as a ten," Star-Lord said. "Let's go for a walk."

When Star-Lord got to the bottom of the tower, he was met with pretty much what he expected: an all-out brawl.

The Thandrid were holding down the ground floor of the tower, many of them in bad shape but still fighting. Groot and a few of the Incarnadinian rebels had made it inside, but most of the fight was happening outside.

"Groot!" Star-Lord called, running down the stairs and into the main action, popping a Thandrid with his quad blaster while dragging Z'Drut along with the other arm. "Nest me, buddy!"

Groot smacked a Thandrid out of the way, and reached for Star-Lord. Just as before, Groot's arm wrapped around Star-Lord in a cocoon of leaves and branches, shielding him from the attacking Thandrid as they moved toward the exit.

"Drones are down!" Star-Lord said. "Go, go, go!"

Groot smashed through the entrance, taking a bit of the siding with him as he brought Star-Lord out into the battlefield. Z'Drut stretched his neck up in Star-Lord's grasp to see. He let out a weak laugh.

"You have ruined me . . . only to step into your own ruin," Z'Drut said. "My wall will rise again, but you . . ."

Star-Lord looked at the scene before him, and couldn't help but fear that the wicked emperor was right. Gamora, Groot, Rocket, Drax, Jesair, the rebels, and the prisoners were locked in vicious combat with the Thandrid protecting the now-dark tower, and they were outnumbered five to one. In the distance, from all directions, more Thandrid were coming.

Star-Lord brought up his quad blaster again and, leaping out of Groot's arm with Z'Drut in tow, let off shot after shot at the Thandrid. He backed up until he was near Gamora.

"You did it," she said, but he could see the worry darkening her gaze. If Gamora was worried, he knew that he was correct to be scared as well.

"You're alive," he said, trying to keep his tone light. "I didn't see you behind me. I thought . . ."

"Got caught up," Gamora said, slashing her blade at a nearby Thandrid. "Ran into Coldios and Jujuine, helped them out of a nasty situation."

"They're alive," Star-Lord said, launching another shot. "That's awesome."

"For now," Z'Drut hissed.

Star-Lord squeezed his arm on the emperor's neck, gritting his teeth as the Thandrid pressed in. He pressed his back against Gamora's as she lashed out with her sword and he let off shot after shot.

"What's our move?" he asked.

"Like you said, Peter. We fight."

He nodded. As the Thandrid got closer and he could no longer see his other friends, he let Z'Drut go and pulled out his laser blaster, shooting now with both hands. Z'Drut fell in a lump on the ground next to him, looking up at Star-Lord with a gleam in his eye as the enemy aliens closed in on them.

"Peter," Gamora said.

Star-Lord's breath caught as he heard her say his name. As far as last things a guy could hear, someone as amazing as Gamora saying his name in that way ranked pretty damn high.

"*Look*," she said. "Above."

Star-Lord didn't have to look up, though. His field of vision was taken over by a flash of blinding purple energy. He shielded his eyes, confused as the Thandrid in front of him froze.

"What?" Z'Drut barked. "What's this?"

The Thandrid, all of them, began to float in the air, still as dolls. Star-Lord watched as they were lifted up by the violet rays that extended back to the gigantic Nova Corps ships congregated in the sky above the battlefield.

Star-Lord's face broke into a brilliant smile, and he turned around to Gamora, who stared in stunned silence as the Thandrid were taken, in stasis, into the Nova Corps ship. Star-Lord threw his arms around Gamora, who squeezed him tightly.

"Holy crap," he said. "We just lived through, like . . . certain death. And I know we've experienced certain death before, but that—that was super, super certain death."

"Hey," Gamora said, patting his back. "I promised, didn't I?"

"You know," Rocket said, striding over to Star-Lord and Gamora as they parted. He jerked his head up to the sky. "I can't say I've ever been happy to see Nova before, but that— that I don't mind too much."

As the Thandrid disappeared into the depths of the Nova Corps ship, and some of the smaller shuttles began to make their landing, sounding a piercing siren, Star-Lord glanced across the battlefield. Drax, bleeding from multiple wounds, stood off to the side, watching as Jesair gathered the Incarnadinians, rebels and prisoners alike, together. He looked over to Star-Lord, met his gaze, and nodded. Star-Lord smiled back at him. Groot was lumbering over to join Star-Lord, Rocket, and Gamora, shaking some remaining exoskeleton out of his bark.

As the Nova Corps soldiers ran out of the shuttles, most certainly armed with as many questions as weapons, Star-Lord felt a sudden wave of relief.

"It's really over, you guys," he said as Drax broke away from the crowd and joined them.

"Over?" Rocket said incredulously. "Are you kidding?"

Star-Lord raised a brow. "Uh, no?"

"Over my freakin' tail," Rocket snapped. "Let's not forget the reason we came here to begin with."

"Dude," Star-Lord said.

Gamora shook his head. "Rocket, really?"

"Cash *money*," Rocket said, rubbing his paws together. "No matter what, I'm not leaving this solar system before we collect!"

Star-Lord patted Rocket on the back. "You know, I love to see some real personal growth in my friends. Really warms the heart."

EPILOGUE

Sanctuary

Four days after the battle on Spiralite, the Guardians of the Galaxy were healed up and ready to leave the solar system and all of its problems behind. They had spent those four days of recuperation on Incarnadine, where the Nova Corps had set up a temporary base while figuring out how to handle the remaining problem of the Thandrid infestation on Bojai and their still-considerable force on Spiralite. Queen Jesair had offered her full cooperation to the Nova Corps, so that together they could gather the remaining Thandrid spawn and ship them all off to the prison planet they'd been sentenced to for their actions in violation of more codes than could be counted.

Star-Lord himself was glad that he and his friends were finally leaving, though he admitted he'd miss the sustenance drink. A beverage that healed his countless wounds while also giving him a buzz and making things all glowy was A-okay in his book.

It was Groot, Star-Lord noticed, who seemed sad to leave

the planet. Since returning, Groot had spent a great deal of time conversing with Queen Jesair, King Irn, and many other Incarnadinians, enjoying a depth of conversation he sure didn't get anywhere else. Drax, though, had become distant from them all, spending the daytime hours taking long walks through the city and staring up at the brilliant, rainbow rings that arced through the skyline.

Drax, Star-Lord knew, was leaving something special behind on this planet. He didn't seem to react toward this like he normally would, though—which was by hitting things. Drax was quiet, but he didn't seem upset. It was almost as if he was allowing himself to take in what he could of the planet while he had the chance, walking through the ruined cities that, in time, would be rebuilt, reflecting on all that had been lost. And, oddly enough, what had been found as well.

Gamora and Rocket were getting antsy, though, and together they'd decided that this was the morning on which they'd leave. Rocket wasn't happy that the Nova Corps told them that, no, of *course* they weren't being paid—but they did reimburse them for their expenses incurred in transporting the medication, which was more than enough to get them on their way. Rocket had started to threaten the officer who told them that's all he was authorized to offer, but Star-Lord had whisked him away before he could say anything that would get them imprisoned.

Who was imprisoned, though, was Z'Drut. Seeing the Nova Corps officers arrest the little tyrant was gratifying, but part of Star-Lord wished he could stick around to witness that particular bit of karma. It was one thing to know that the wicked emperor would be tried and sentenced harshly for his part in the genocide, but it was another to *see* it happen.

Star-Lord knew, though, that his life would be better if neither he nor any of his friends ever saw Emperor Z'Drut again.

As the sun set on Incarnadine that night, the Guardians of the Galaxy gathered around the *Milano*, which the rebel mechanics had graciously repaired and stocked full of their sustenance beverage. They shared good-byes with Coldios, Jujuine, King Irn, and the other rebels with whom they'd spent the last few days, along with a group of the prisoners who were currently residing on Incarnadine, waiting for Nova transport back to their home planets.

Jesair parted from the group of Incarnadinians, joining the Guardians of the Galaxy near the open port of the ship.

"I can't thank you enough," she said, looking at each of them. "Without your guidance, bravery, and power, my once beautiful home would've become a graveyard. I owe you my life, but I give you my heart."

"Trust me," Gamora said, taking Jesair's hands in her own. "We would've been in equally bad shape without you. You owe us nothing."

Jesair moved on to Star-Lord, who grinned at her. She grasped his hands in her warm grip, holding them for a moment as she stared at him with fondness. "Gamora is wise, but I disagree. Incarnadine owes a debt to all of you . . . but perhaps most of all to you, Peter Quill. Take my gratitude, and drink deeply of our sustenance. I know you enjoy it."

"That I do," Star-Lord said. "Oh, and hey . . . listen, if you ever get an update on what they're doing with Z'Drut, could you pop us a comm and let us know? Really hate that guy."

"He is, as you said over last night's dinner, a fart-waffle," Jesair said, which made Rocket chortle.

Jesair bent down to Rocket, who grinned at her, lifting up his lips to reveal a set of tiny fangs. "My brave friend," she said, rubbing his shoulder. "I know you are disappointed in the results of your trip to Bojai . . . but perhaps I have something to offer that could lift your spirits."

Rocket's eyes widened. "Enough money to crush me?" he asked.

"Not quite," Jesair said. "A job for the Guardians of the Galaxy. There is a planet not far from here that has reached out in hopes of hiring a transport team. They are a race of gelatinous immortals on a modest but peaceful planet called Putriline—"

"Ugh," Rocket said, sneering.

"Ohhhh no," Star-Lord said. "Nope. No, nope."

"I am Groot," Groot said, shaking his head.

"Oh!" Jesair said, her eyes flashing with surprise. "I see! Perhaps, you'd like a rest, then. I empathize with that."

"Yes," Gamora said, chuckling as she jabbed Star-Lord in the ribs with her elbow. "*That*'s why."

Jesair moved on to Groot, who embraced her in a leafy hug. When they parted, he held out his hand, which blossomed with white flowers that matched the color of her sparkling eyes. "I am Groot," he said, smiling warmly as he placed the flowers in her hair.

"Thank you, my dear friend," Jesair said. "And please remember . . . you are not only as others see you. You are you, always."

Finally, she moved to Drax. Drax opened his mouth to speak, but Jesair just looked at him, eye to eye, silently. They stood for a moment, until Jesair took a step toward him and rested her face against his chest. He held out his arms, as if to embrace her, but shifted around, unsure of where to place them.

"Peace," she said softly, parting from Drax. "You have brought it back to my life. I wish it, in every form it comes, for you. We share a piece of soul, Drax. Remember that."

Drax nodded, his eyes shining.

That made Star-Lord smile.

Jesair watched them as they loaded onto the ship. Within moments, they were situated, lifting off of the ground. They gathered on the flight deck, with Star-Lord sitting in the pilot's seat this time and Rocket next to him. Between them, Gamora was working the touch-screen map, picking their next destination. Groot and Drax stood in the distance, quiet. Incarnadine disappeared in their view finder along with Bojai and then, in time, Spiralite as well. They flew past the area that had once been the drone wall and shifted into light speed, flying forward into the blackness of space.

"Where to?" Star-Lord said, glancing at Gamora.

She grinned at him. "You know? I have no idea."

"I am Groot," Groot spoke up from the back.

"I agree with him," Rocket said. "Freakin' *anywhere* but Putriline."

"Drax?" Star-Lord said, looking back at his burly buddy, who was gazing out of the tempered-glass nose of the ship into the starry depths before them. "Any ideas?"

"Yes," Drax said, his voice quieter than Star-Lord had ever heard him speak. He breathed out, and then smiled. "I'd just like to fly for a while."

"Absolutely can do," Star-Lord said, pulling back the gear before him, and then turned around to face his friends as the ship shot off to nowhere in particular. He got up and joined Drax as they stared out at the endless tapestry of stars and planets before them.

"My wife . . ." Drax started, looking out at the view. "She would stare up at the stars, long before I set out into space myself. She used to say that knowing how much life was out there made her feel so small. In comparison to the larger universe—not physically smaller than her normal stature."

"Yep," Star-Lord said. "I got that part."

"I think, in time, she might have changed her mind, though," Drax said.

"What do you mean?" Star-Lord asked.

"I don't feel small when I look out at these worlds anymore," Drax said, looking from Star-Lord, to Groot, to Rocket, to Gamora, and then back out to the dazzling view. He shook his head. "I feel as if, finally, I'm not alone."

ACKNOWLEDGMENTS

Picture this. I'm at a Thanksgiving dinner at my brother's house. My mom is asking if my sister-in-law needs help serving, my fiancée Amy is telling my father a story, and the family dog, Baker, is shoving his face into everyone's legs beneath the table. My phone buzzes with an email and I casually glance at it as the turkey is placed in the center of the table. When I see what that email says, though . . . I'm stunned. It's an invite from Deanna McFadden to write a Guardians of the Galaxy novel.

I'd like to imagine that I kept it cool, but I'm sure if we looked back at that email thread, my response was closer to "Hell, yeah!" than a calm, measured acceptance.

The Guardians of the Galaxy have taken the world by storm in recent years, and if you saw the film, you know exactly why. They're irreverent, interesting, emotionally nuanced, and three-dimensional characters in an equally nuanced world that is full of whimsy, wonder, and aliens so strange that looking at them might break your mind. What's most interesting about the Guardians to me isn't the gothic juxtaposition of putting these vulgar and hilarious characters in the epic setting of a space opera. I mean, sure, that works well enough, but by the time we catch up with our heroes, they're pretty damn epic themselves. What makes the Guardians of the Galaxy the definitive spacefaring heroes of our time is their humanity. Their tale is a comedy, a tragedy, a philosophical morality play, a fart joke, a redemptive bildungsroman, and a war story all in one . . . and, as funny as it gets, it feels by my estimation closer to the way real life is than most of the science fiction I've seen.

People are funny, even in the midst of tragedy. People are inconsistent, they don't say what they actually feel or think, they're reactive, and they're messy. *Guardians of the Galaxy* is ALL about that. So I have to give due props to James Gunn, Nicole Perlman, and Kevin Feige for their work on the film, without which this novel would be a hell of a lot different. Also, a big shout-out to Guardians creators Dan Abnett and Andy Lanning, without whom neither the book nor film would exist at all.

I had a great deal of fun playing around in the cosmic sector of the Marvel universe. I can't thank Marvel and Joe Books enough for the chance to take these characters I love and throw them into a life-threatening circumstance. (Writers are pretty messed up, aren't we?) Steve Osgoode, Deanna McFadden, Michael Melgaard, Emma Hambly, Rebecca Mills, and the entire Joe Books team are a huge part of why this book is a thing. I am forever grateful to their dedication and general awesomeness.

I hope you enjoyed *Space Riot* as much as I enjoyed writing it. Because dang, that was fun. If I had to sum up the novel in a single phrase, cheesy as it is, it'd be this: "If fear leads you to build walls, the Guardians of the Galaxy are going to come and pop the sacs of your clam-faced allies."

That's how themes work, right?

Pat Shand
April 2017

ABOUT THE AUTHOR

PAT SHAND writes comics (*Destiny NY, Shut Eye, Vampire Emmy & the Garbage Girl*), novels (*Marvel Iron Man: Mutually Assured Destruction, Marvel Avengers: The Serpent Society, Charmed: Social Medium, Charmed: Symphony for the Devil*), and more. He lives in New York with his fiancée Amy and their zoo of cats. Follow him @PatShand pretty much everywhere.